CALL OF THE SEA

BY

CAPTAIN RON SMITH

TABLE OF CONTENTS

Foreword 1

Chapter I: Freeport Or Bust....................................8

Chapter 2: Falling For The Sea 20

Chapter 3: Lifeguard Days 33

Chapter 4: The Party Island..................................50

Chapter 5: Fish Tales 66

Chapter 6: Meeting Cyndi.....................................81

Chapter 7: Carving Out A Kingdom 96

Chapter 8: First Mate For Life 105

Chapter 9: Dark Days And New Beginnings 122

Chapter 10: A New Way To Make A Living 146

Chapter 11: Seafaring Friends And Comfort Foods..........................158

Chapter 12: Adventures In Boating......................171

Chapter 13: Battling The Elements 204

Chapter 14: Legacies And Reflections................218

Fisherman's Prayer 224

FOREWORD

I've known Ron and Cyndi for almost 30 years. Boating with him every season with my wife of over 60 years, Flora. I met Ron and Cyndi at my 60th birthday party; I am now 86 and love boats the same way Flora and I did 50 years ago. Ron and Cyndi were usually the leaders on any trip we went on with them. Their confidence and experience made me and others that traveled with them very calm, even in heavy fog, which Rhode Island and New England have quite often. If there was any anxiety in their travels because of fog or seas or caught in storms, we never saw it. I was very happy when they were planning their next chapter in life by moving to Florida. They planned it for a few years. Ron worked on how to sell his residential development business and his land, to move on June 1, 2019. Cyndi was a very accomplished loan officer with the same bank for over 20 years. She got a job with a bank in Florida before the move, and Ron had his real estate broker license transferred to Florida—a license he had since 1985. He took a little longer to move because he had to finish a few homes under construction. Ron did real estate sales for one year or so in Florida but was burned out after 37 years in the business. He had a lot of hours in boats under his belt and decided to do a job with the six-pack captain's license and work for a company doing nature tours, taxi services, boating instruction, and anything the customer or company required. That wasn't enough for him. He needed to experience the open ocean again as he did in New England. He worked to get his 25-ton, 50-ton, and now with his 100-ton license, he can choose the boats he wants to deliver to far off places. This is what he was meant to do. He knows how to handle a boat, and I would trust him anywhere.

Tony Simeone

Tony and Flora Simeone, every boater's friends.
I want to be them when I grow up.

PREFACE

I came about writing this book because of my love of the sea. From a young boy about 13 years old, I had a calling to the water, residential development, and real estate. I was very good at all of them and loved them all very much. I rose through the ranks of my real estate career. There were many times that I thought my career was just a way to gain money for this very expensive boating endeavor. It was at 13 that my parents moved to Narragansett, Rhode Island from Western Massachusetts, so my father could take over my grandfather's cobbler business. I found the beach very exciting and new. I was there almost every sunny day to play in the waves, learn to boogie board, and try to learn surfing, which I never really conquered. About the same time, I met my close friend Dean, who lived only two streets away. We both loved the beach, and he introduced me to boats. His father was an old "Swamp Yankee" fisherman, and he let Dean take his boat out before school. We would scallop in the morning, shuck them after school, and sell them to local restaurants before dinner time. We would also go clamming, water ski, and just play on the boat for hours when not in school. I bought my first boat, a 13-foot Boston Whaler, soon after. My Father restored old shoes, pocketbooks, leather jackets, and any other leather goods that needed to be repaired. He worked very hard to give us a good life but also taught us the 13 value of a dollar. If we wanted something, we were told not to ask for it, but to get out and work to save the money for it—a great value I still have today. With those words of wisdom, I was a lifeguard, bartender, realtor, and home developer, but my biggest joy was to be on a boat. Traveling, exploring, and navigating were the things that made me the happiest. I would read about boating and how to repair and winterize them. Before we moved to Florida in 2019, I had about 7000 hours on the water from dozens of boating trips; now I have over 8000. Cyndi is a truly amazing woman who always encouraged me to follow my dreams, and she never held me back. I had a financially rewarding career, nice cars, boats, a waterfront home in Rhode Island, and an investment waterfront home in Florida. Something kept calling me though, and I didn't figure it out until we moved to Florida. There were many people there making a living from water-centric tourist attractions. I decided to pivot my career and received only encouragement from Cyndi. I first obtained my six-pack captain's license and got a great job with a small company on North Captiva Island. I piloted a water taxi, ran guided nature tours of dolphin and manatee habitats, and taught boating to many Midwesterners who didn't have any experience with handling a boat on the ocean. I started hearing about captains delivering yachts all over the Atlantic coast. This opportunity would definitely meet my needs and desire to be on the open water. I had so many hours skippering yachts and boats, I knew there was not a vessel I couldn't handle or a sea I couldn't figure out how and CALL OF THE SEA 14 value of a dollar. If we wanted something, we were told not to ask for it, but to get out and work to save the money for it—a great value I still have today. With those words of wisdom, I was a lifeguard, bartender, realtor, and home developer, but my biggest joy was to be on a boat. Traveling, exploring, and navigating were the things that made me the happiest. I would read about boating and how to repair and winterize them. Before we moved to Florida in 2019, I had about 7000 hours on the water from dozens of boating trips; now I have over 8000. Cyndi is a truly amazing woman who always encouraged me to follow my dreams, and she never held me back. I had a financially rewarding career, nice cars, boats, a waterfront home in Rhode Island, and an investment waterfront home in Florida. Something kept calling me though, and I didn't figure it out until we moved to Florida. There were many people there making a living from water-centric tourist attractions. I decided to pivot my career and received only encouragement from Cyndi. I first obtained my six-pack captain's license and got a great job with a small company on North Captiva Island. I piloted a water taxi, ran guided nature tours of dolphin and manatee habitats, and taught boating to many Midwesterners who didn't have any experience with handling a boat on the ocean. I started hearing about captains delivering yachts all over the Atlantic coast. This opportunity would definitely meet my needs and desire to be on the open water. I had so many hours skippering yachts and boats, I knew there was not a vessel I couldn't handle or a sea I couldn't figure out how and CALL OF THE SEA 14 when to traverse, depending on weather conditions. I worked hard to obtain my 25-ton, 50-ton, and eventually my goal of a 100-ton Captain's license. I have worked at several careers and jobs, and I fully enjoyed all of them, but how does one know if those chosen jobs or careers are the ones that will truly provide the fulfillment needed? We all have abilities and interests, but sometimes we are not interested in what we can do or the interest. How do we align interests and ability? Nothing occurs at one point in time, it occurs over a span of time. The story you are about to read is a timeline of my life and events that changed myself, my wife, and our lives. I deliver yachts from 30 to 100 feet up to Maine and to the Keys, the Bahamas, and the Caribbean. All the coming chapters, even the ones that don't seem like I love the ocean, are a tribute to my girl, the open ocean. The sea has finally wholly captured me. I am thoroughly happy and enjoy every day I'm doing it.

Captain Ron Smith

CHAPTER I:
FREEPORT OR BUST

The ocean has always been my greatest love, but she demands respect. You're at her mercy when you're out on the open water, miles from land. I've never felt this more acutely than on a trip to Freeport, Bahamas. It started with a call from a Canadian gentleman who'd been spending time with his wife on his 48-foot Jefferson Yacht, the Orion, down in the Keys. Originally from Ontario, they'd been enjoying the Florida coast for a couple of years now. But his father-in-law lived over in Freeport, and they wanted to bring the boat to him. The yacht was docked in Marathon Key, which is halfway to Key West, but we were on the coast of the Gulf of Mexico, so we had to take her around. We found our way up Hawks Channel, a small channel between the Keys and the nasty rocky area that guards the passageway from the channel to the open ocean. It's slow going in such an unforgiving landscape, so it took us all the morning and most of the afternoon to get north to Miami.

This might be a good time to mention that you better know what you're doing before taking a trip across the Florida Straits. Those winds can whip the seas into a frenzy that'll make even seasoned captains queasy. But I'd made the crossing plenty of times before and knew I could handle it. The key is preparation. "Corey," I called to my first mate as we readied the *Orion* at the dock in Miami. "Make sure those fuel tanks are topped off. The last thing we need is to run out of fuel halfway to Bimini."

"Already on it, captain," she replied with a mock salute. Corey and I had been working together for a while. She was one of my best deckhands—she anticipated what needed doing and did it without being asked. She even had a few choice sailor words once in a while. A Damn, Shit or Hell correctly placed would make me grin. A captain couldn't ask for better than that.

I've found over the years that licensed female mates are the best to have. They work harder because it's a male-dominated field, they listen to the captain better than their male counterparts, and they are less likely to walk off the boat if they don't agree. What can I say? Women are better at being deckhands. As we guided the *Orion* through the drawbridges, out of the Keys, and past Biscayne Bay, I noticed an unusual amount of traffic in the waters around Miami. The cruise ships were lined up one after the other, departing the Port of Miami like gussied-up ladies off to a fancy ball. Their lights twinkled like Christmas trees against the dimming afternoon sky. I checked my watch: 4 p.m. We had maybe three hours of daylight left, plenty of time to get a good way across the Straits before dark. We decided to make a full 24-hour run, pulling an all-nighter. The seas and wind were just right, favorable and with not a cloud in the sky, and the moon shimmered overhead, beautiful and blue. I couldn't ask for anything more, except that the sea and the ship kept us safe with no breakdowns.

I settled into a heading and pushed the throttle forward. The engines purred as the *Orion* cut through the small swells.

About two hours out, the lights of Miami only a distant glow on the horizon some 12 miles behind us, I heard a strange sound off the starboard side. A kind of whooshing puff. I cut the engines to idle and leaned over the rail, peering into the blue. To my shock, an enormous eye stared back at me, attached to a small whale's sleek gray and white head. Well, small for a whale—this thing was still nearly as big as our 48-foot boat, and its eye alone was the size of a baseball. It regarded me placidly for a long moment, then, with a flex of its powerful tail, vanished back beneath the waves.

I gasped. In all my years on the water I'd seen plenty of marine life but never had a close encounter quite like that. Shaking my head with a smile on my face, I pushed the *Orion* back up to speed. We hit the Gulf Stream, and I watched our speed jump from seven knots to 11 as the current grabbed us and pulled us along. I kept a close eye on the charts and GPS, minding our course. This far out, it'd be all too easy to drift off track. The flywheel of the starboard engine started slipping a lot. This meant I needed to bring that engine to idle or risk frying it from the heat, but gremlins like these always show up to try and ruin things. You must know how to pivot. Corey had gone below deck to grab some shuteye before her shift at the wheel. Alone with my thoughts, I sipped a coffee, the bitter bite helping offset the fatigue of a long day, and scanned the darkening horizon. About 15 minutes after the first gremlin threatened our journey, I spotted the running lights of a massive cargo freighter off in the distance, probably heading for the busy industrial port in Freeport.

I reached over and flipped on our own running lights, not wanting to change the cargo freighter, not seeing our smaller craft and cutting across our path, but the DC circuits shut down. That meant our running lights, the VHF radio, and all the other electronics, except for one, went dark. For some unknown reason, the owner ran the wire directly to the battery when installing the GPS. Fortunately, the one item we needed most was working fine, but we had no lights. That was a disaster waiting to happen. I ran down to get my ditch bag, which I carry on every trip. I pulled out the new Coast Guard-approved hand-held extra, extra bright lights and a bunch of zip ties, and then I hung the emergency lights where the regular ones should have been and returned to my peaceful stargazing. That's just the sort of thing you must be ready for in the open water. The ocean's a harsh mistress; she'll kill you in a heartbeat if you don't respect her power.

There were all kinds of ships heading the same direction as us, too—tankers, cargo carriers, and the occasional cruise ship lit up like

Christmas trees. This might be a good time to mention that when boats are brought to the Keys and Bahamas, they're often brought there to die. There's a saying, "When boats are brought to the Keys and Bahamas, many times they're brought there to die, and they're never coming back." So, the cherry on top was that Orion was probably destined for the same fate—and there I was, in that same boat, in the middle of nowhere. And if you've ever had the pleasure of navigating through Florida's waters, you'll understand how inhospitable the state can be if you catch it at the wrong time. Currents running north at about 4 to 5 knots are not to be messed with. And if there's a wind from the North coming in, you could be staring down 11–12-foot waves in the blink of an eye. Thankfully, I got lucky, and nature decided to have mercy on me, and I felt the guard was with me. But the boat itself? Well, that's a different story. The engine was glitching, the electrical system was falling apart, and the boat became completely dysfunctional somewhere along the line, leaving me stranded in the middle of the ocean in the dark. Right when I was smack in the middle of a channel the strait, surrounded by cruise ships, big yachts, and cargo ships. But of all the things to happen, I got seen by a whale.

And let me tell you, it was breathtaking. There are no words that can truly capture what I felt. No bigger description, no matter how grand could ever summarize the sheer mesmerization that washed over me when I saw that whale. It was a fleeting moment, probably only lasting four seconds, but the impact? It was surely Monumental. It felt like time slowed down, stretching those brief moments into what seemed like ten minutes, every second heavy with wonder. The whale was about 35 feet long—smaller than my boat, which was 48 feet, but size didn't matter. It approached, its massive body cutting through the water, then it paused—looked up at me, almost curiously. It was as if it was assessing the boat, like it was deciding whether or not to come closer. And in that moment, I felt something stirring deep inside me. I had spent so much time on the sea, so many years immersed in it, that I didn't feel like a man in a boat in those seconds. I felt like part of the ocean—the salt, the waves, the vastness. The whale and I weren't strangers. We were equals. I couldn't say for sure what kind of whale it was, but I have this gut feeling it was a minke whale. The sea is full of mysteries, after all—secrets it keeps locked away, like the minke whale, and the others we don't even know about. What lies beneath the surface, only God knows—and honestly, I'd like to leave it that way.

But in the back of my mind, something dark crept in a rush of intrusive thoughts, each one more terrifying than the last. I feared for my life, yet, strangely, I made peace with it. I thought to myself, "This could be my last day on the water." That whale's mother might come charging through the waves, crushing me, my boat, everything into an unrecognizable heap. The thought gripped me. But then, I saw those eyes... those eyes... They were the size of baseballs—huge and full of something ancient, something unfathomable. And they just looked at me, still and unwavering, like they were saying, "Yeah, I see you."

At that moment, I didn't feel afraid anymore. I felt small, yes, but also chosen like I was witnessing something only the few who are truly meant to see it get to. And I'm haunted by it still. That eye. I don't think I'll ever forget it. It feels like yesterday.

By that time, the boat had become truly dysfunctional, but I had to "let there be light" through that situation, so I waited there, staring out at the horizon, fantasizing about what kind of whale I had just encountered. It was fully dark by the time the lights of Freeport appeared off our bow. Corey and I decided it was wiser to wait outside the narrow channel, with rocks on both sides, especially on only one engine until sun up to navigate through it. We each got some shuteye, but when the sun started coming over the horizon too soon after I laid down my weary head, we answered the call and started our entry. I throttled back and carefully navigated the unfamiliar channel markers, not wanting to arrive at Customs with a dinged-up hull. "Where do we go?" Corey asked, rubbing sleep from her eyes as she emerged into the cockpit. "Well, the funny thing about the Bahamas, apparently Immigration and Customs are two different offices here," I said. "Gotta do Immigration first, then take the boat over to the Customs dock."

She quirked an eyebrow in confusion but just shrugged. "You're the captain."

As we tied off at the Immigration dock, I couldn't help but notice the half dozen other boats that had arrived right behind us. It looked like everyone had the same idea about getting across the Straits that night.

We all shuffled onto the dock and lined up under the flickering fluorescent lights of the Immigration building. An hour ticked by. Then two. My stomach started to growl, and I regretted not grabbing dinner before we left Miami. Finally, the customs lady arrived, late, of course. And by the twinkle in her eye, I could tell there was something more than just checking documents going on. She rounded us up and asked, "Okay, nobody has any fruits or vegetables they shouldn't be carrying, right?" Now, it's funny because who doesn't have fruits, veggies, and a bit of sandwich meat on their boat? We all just stared at her, trying to act innocent, and then she dropped a bombshell. "And nobody has any firearms on them, right?" She winked in a way that goes, *"I know you all know, and I know you know that I know."* I was a little nervous because it's illegal to bring a weapon through customs in the Bahamas, but there's a lot of piracy around, so that's why they're so strict. The lady's twinkling eyes said it all. She looked us over, then said with a sly grin, "I could go through every single one of your boats, but if you all look at me and nod your heads, yes, I'll pass every one of you." Naturally, we all nodded our heads and laughed, and just like that, we were stamped and cleared through. Thank God I didn't have to throw out my gun, my sandwich meat, or my apples and fruits. Speaking of fruits, an old sailor says you should never bring bananas on a boat because it's bad luck. So, you guessed it—we didn't bring any bananas, that one rule we surely followed.

"Well, that was easy," I thought to myself, eager to get the apples, pears, cold cuts, and bread out of their hiding spots. We didn't want to throw out good food if we didn't need to. With a whoop of relief, we practically flew through Immigration, eager to get tied off for the night and find ourselves some grub and a cold Kalik to wash away the salt. I let Corey steer us over to the Customs slip while I dug out the ship's papers. We docked right alongside a boat I recognized from Miami— the owner gave me a tired wave, and I returned it in commiseration. It had been a long night on the water for all of us.

After getting cleared, I carefully spun the wheel and aimed the bow of the *Orion* toward the slip the owner had described to me. It was a tricky maneuver—a serpentine path carved between coral heads, requiring the boat to zig left and then back to the right like some waterborne obstacle course. Of course, Murphy's Law decided to rear its head at that moment—the starboard engine sputtered and died, leaving us only the port prop to navigate with. I muttered some choice words and worked the throttles, trying to coax the *Orion* into the slip without bashing into any of the very expensive-looking yachts to either side. To my relief and, judging by the clapping and whooping from the small crowd observing on the dock, theirs as well, I managed to bring the old girl in without so much as a scratch.

As I hopped onto the weathered planks, the owner rushed over and enthusiastically pumped my hand. "I knew you could do it, captain! When I saw that engine quit, I thought I was going to have to dive in myself," he joked. I accepted his praise as graciously as I could, secretly just happy to finally have solid ground under my feet again. As much as I love the ocean, I need a break from her every now and then. "Happy to have her here all in one piece, sir," I said. "Now, any recommendations on where a weary sailor might find a good meal around here?"

His grin widened as he pointed towards the twinkling lights of the marina's outdoor bar. "Right over there are some of the best conch fritters you'll ever taste. Welcome to Freeport."

As Corey and I ambled over to the bar, cold drinks already in hand, I breathed in the sweet scent of hibiscus on the evening breeze and smiled. The old girl had gotten us here safe once again. Another successful dance with my first mistress, the sea.

I raised my bottle in a silent toast.

"Until the next voyage, my dear. Until the next voyage."

48-foot Freeman trawler, The Orion, ending in dock in Freeport

A small (35-foot) whale like this one eyeing me and our boat in the Florida Straits.

Waiting till sunup outside Freeport, Bahamas.
Cruise ships waiting too. Lit up like Christmas trees.

CHAPTER 2:
FALLING FOR THE SEA

The day we moved to Rhode Island; my whole world turned upside down. There I was, this scrawny 13-year-old kid straight out of Western Massachusetts, not knowing what the hell I was in for. I had no idea what was about to unfold, but little did I know that nature would become my greatest teacher. Then came the life-changing event when I laid eyes on the Atlantic Ocean for the first time. The sound of the waves crashing against the shore, the smell of the salty air, and the feel of the sand between my toes was all so overwhelming. It was as if the Earth was welcoming me, and I felt truly alive for the first time. With her endless horizon, the ocean seemed to speak a language I hadn't yet learned, but I understood it all the same. The ocean that I saw wasn't just water and waves for me; it was a living, breathing thing that called to me, like an old friend who knew me better than I knew myself, and I definitely shook hands with it like, "Yeah, I'm in. I surrender." It all felt like a destiny, as if I had been waiting for this moment my entire life. And there you have it, boom, I was a goner, head over heels in love. The second I felt that sand between my toes and took a deep breath of that briny air, I knew she had me for life. The ocean reached out and snatched my heart that day, and I've been her willing prisoner ever since, helpless in her vast, mysterious arms.

Sure, I'd seen the ocean before on television. But for a kid from the sticks like me, it was just a big puddle you drove by on the way to mini golf and clam strips. I never felt that pull, you know? That "come hither," the sea whispers in your ear, luring you in until you can't think about anything else. When I finally stood before it, I felt something stir deep inside me, an instinctual knowing, like the ocean had always been a part of me even though it was so unfamiliar to me at that time. But how can someone not get lost in the wilderness of the waves and the unpredictability of it? It all felt sacred, like nature had painted a surreal masterpiece for me to navigate through and sway with the sounds of nature. The kind of pull made you want to get lost in her vastness, surrender to her beauty. When I finally heard her sultry voice that summer, it set off a hunger in me, I didn't even know was there. I wanted to dive into those waves and figure out what made them tick, to learn all of her secrets. I had to know everything about her, as if I had discovered a new world, a world I was meant to explore and cherish.

From that day on, good luck trying to drag me away from the beach. If I wasn't in school or getting nagged to do chores, you'd find me down by the shore. I was in that water as the sun came up most mornings, roughhousing with my buddies in the surf. We'd push each other off the jetties, chuck seaweed at each other's heads, just being total knuckleheads. Even in our wild, carefree ways, we were grounded by something deeper, a sense of connection to the ocean that bound us together. We weren't just kids playing in the waves—we were part of the rhythm of the sea, caught in its eternal dance. Man… we were happy. Even now, I can tell you this— You give a pack of teenage boys some waves and a few beat-up boogie boards, and you'll find them in hog heaven. The joy of the moment, the pull of the ocean, pure, unfiltered, and endless.

I couldn't get enough of it. Pretty soon, I was checking out the lifeguards, these real buff dudes perched up there in their towers like they owned the place. They were total rock stars to 13-year-old me. I thought, "That's it; that's what I want to be when I grow up." If guarding the beach meant I could live in my swimsuit and never be far from my one true love, sign me up. The idea of being so close to the ocean, feeling its constant presence, was intoxicating. Like you're telling me I can sit here under the embrace of the majesty of ocean waves as a job? Sure, sign me up right now, no questions asked. It's safe to say that there was something about the way the sea stretched out endlessly, offering a sense of freedom and connection that filled me with a longing so ecstatic. To be part of that, to protect it, to have a life so intertwined with nature, seemed like the perfect dream.

Before long, I purchased my first boat, a 13-foot Boston Whaler. I was 14 and couldn't wait to get out on the water. As often as possible, I would take her out to Point Judith Pond, scalloping, snorkeling, water skiing, and general joy riding. I would do anything to be on the water. It was just one of those things I couldn't shake, that constant pull toward the waves. The sea had a way of calling to me, always reminding me that I was never truly home unless I was surrounded by its vastness. I'd take that boat anywhere – it was perfect for the pond, where we would hunt for scallops and have a blast on the water. I was in heaven, surrounded by the beauty of the water, the sunlight dancing on its surface, and the sounds of nature whispering all around me.

I'm getting a little carried away in this "flood" of emotions which leads me to the next point. No matter who I was or how much my heart was filled with the love of the sea, there's one thing nobody can deny: the nature is brutal, and if you want to work with it—you have to inevitably embrace its ruthless glory. The ocean had to knock me around a bit first, and teach me some manners before I could start taking care of other people in her waters. Fair enough, how would I rescue anybody else if I can't save myself in the depths of such vastness? So, she tossed me like dirty laundry in the washing machine plenty of times during the first couple years, to the point that I experienced an ego death and completely submitted myself into its grace. I'd be out there thinking I was big stuff, catching waves on this ancient longboard I'd bought for twenty bucks. Next thing I know, I'm getting pile-driven into the sand, saltwater shooting out my nose and my trunks halfway to Cuba. But if there's one thing the ocean teaches you, it's respect. You don't take her on thinking you'll win—that's a law. You enter the ocean without knowing the laws, and the nature surrounds you with situations where you just have to sit down and abide by those laws. You go in humble, let her push you around some, and eventually, you start to figure out her rhythms—the way she moves, the way she breathes, and the quiet power that lies beneath her surface; all of it.

When I wasn't trying to surf, I was racing catamarans with my buddy John. We'd haul this rickety old cat down to the beach, dragging it over the warm, golden sand, and point her straight out into the big blue. The excitement would build as we pushed off, feeling the salty spray of the ocean on our faces and the adrenaline pumping through our veins. Each gust of wind, each wave that caught us, felt like a part of nature's pulse, its heartbeat echoing in our chests. It was as if we were riding the rhythm of the Earth itself, and the vast and untamed ocean had welcomed us into her world. More than once, I thought we were goners out there getting thrashed by 8-foot swells with no land in sight. The waves would tower overhead, and it felt like we were on a roller coaster, just waiting for the inevitable drop. There was something exhilarating, yet humbling about it—a raw, untamed energy that left us feeling more alive than ever. It was nothing like anything I had ever experienced before. The ocean, both fierce and beautiful, reminded me just how small we were in her vastness. One time, the hull started taking on water, and I was sure we'd be shark bait. The adrenaline kicking your flight and fight instinct while being surrounded by the water is deathly harrowing. The thought of being helpless, vulnerable in the deep blue, with danger lurking below the surface, sent a cold shiver through me. You don't wanna be caught up in a situation where you're counting down the moments until the worst could happen. I still remember like it was yesterday, the image of fins cutting through the surface sending chills down my spine. But John kept his cool; he was a steady presence, even in chaos. He stuffed his t-shirt in the crack, sealing it up like a makeshift patch, and started bailing like a fiend with a plastic jug we always kept on board for emergencies. We trembled with a mix of fear and thrill as we managed to limp her back to shore intact, feeling like we'd spat in the old girl's eye and lived to tell about it. That day was a testament to our reckless courage and the undeniable bond the ocean had forged between us in all her beauty and danger.

If sailing Hobie Cats taught me to stay calm in rough seas, snorkeling is where I truly learned to use my melon. See, my oldest friend Dean and I would spend hours hunting scallops in the shallows, rolling ourselves into wetsuits and gearing up to dive beneath the water's shimmering surface. There was something about the weightlessness of the ocean that made every breath feel like a gift, and every dive, an opportunity to explore the vast beauty below. When the water was too shallow in some areas, we used a hundred-year-old way of gathering scallops, using what's called a window. It's an old wooden box with a glass bottom, for visibility underwater. From inside the boat, which was drifting with the current, we looked through the window, and as the scallops came out of the seagrass, propelling themselves backward, we scooped them up with the net. It felt like a partnership between us and the sea, a quiet dance of patience and precision. Once we got a bushel, we would dock, carry them back to Dean's cold basement for storage, and go to school. After school, we would head to Dean's, shuck the scallops, and place them in quart plastic containers to sell that night to the local restaurants, feeling like kings with each handful of glistening shells. We didn't have permits, so we accepted cash only, and boy, were we money-hungry. The sea had provided, and we were determined to take advantage of it. Sometimes, we would even go out in late November and freeze our butts off just to make a few bucks. As much as I loved the money, I also valued the education. You get to know the underwater terrain well while snorkeling since you're staring at it through a mask day after day, memorizing every crevice and rock formation. I developed a deep connection with that hidden world, learning its secrets, reading its patterns, and respecting its unpredictable nature. I figured out how to read the bottom for where the shellfish liked to hang out, spot the predators lurking in the shadows, and conserve my oxygen when I needed to work a tricky spot for a while. I can still recall the gentle current swirling around me as I navigated the underwater landscape, feeling the thrill of discovery and the quiet serenity of this hidden world. Let's just say it's come in handy once or twice since then when I've found myself in deep water, if you know what I mean. Those lessons in calmness and resourcefulness have served me well beyond those sandy shores. The ocean had taught me more than I realized in those days—lessons in patience, perseverance, and trust that things would reveal themselves when the time was right.

Now, any of you fellas remember what it was like being a 14 or 15-year-old boy at the beach? The sun was always shining, the surf was always calling, and every day felt like an unending adventure. The world was full of possibility, and the beach was the perfect backdrop for all of it. There was an energy in the air, a sense of freedom, that made everything feel like it was waiting for us to explore it. Let me tell you, it wasn't just the waves I was scoping out, you know? The day I realized girls were more interesting than any fish I might wrangle, my whole worldview changed. It was as if a switch flipped, and suddenly, as an older teenager, the ocean wasn't the only thing captivating my attention, and suddenly, I found myself torn between the waves and the laughter of girls on the shore. It's funny now because when I sit down with my wife, I still remember her words when we dated later in college, going, "Ron, you can always look at the menu, you just can't order," and I'd like to hold on to that now. But looking back, I still logged plenty of hours in the water, honing my skills and chasing down the perfect wave, but I was paying attention to the scenery. The laughter of girls echoed around me, and my heart raced a little faster when I caught their eye. It was a new kind of excitement, one that made the salty air feel even sweeter. I recall the nervousness mixed with excitement as I tried to impress them, riding the waves with a little more flair or blushing as I stumbled over my words. Those sun-soaked days were filled with innocent flirtations and the thrill of youthful romance. Each glance felt electric, igniting a spark that made every surf session feel even more exhilarating. I was discovering a new kind of adventure—one that didn't just include the ocean but also the magic of those early crushes, shaping my teenage years into a whirlwind of unforgettable moments. The sea wasn't the only thing that had my heart racing anymore; the world around me had suddenly become much larger, and I was ready to dive in, headfirst. The sound of their laughter and the warmth of the sun on my face became as much a part of the adventure as the waves themselves. The whole world felt alive in those moments, filled with possibilities and the promise of new experiences around every corner.

These gorgeous, tanned creatures would lay out not far from the lifeguard stands, slick with baby oil and not much else. It was like the whole beach was one endless smorgasbord of eye candy. I'd pick my spot carefully, making sure I had a good view of the prettiest ones.

Then I'd strut a little, try to look busy scanning for sharks or Cuban subs or whatever. Really, I was just hoping a certain blonde in a purple bikini might need "saving." I can't tell you how many times I had to snap myself out of a daydream to realize some toddler was heading for open water.

But I got up the nerve to talk to a few beach beauties. Most of the time, they just giggled and rolled their eyes at whatever line I was trying to spit, but occasionally, I'd make a connection. There was this one brunette, man, she was a knock-out. I got her to come watch me at a junior lifeguarding competition one weekend. I was supposed to rescue this practice dummy we called "Lester the Molester" and drag him to shore. It should've been simple, but my nerves were shot. It was probably the worst timing for a rookie mistake. Well, wouldn't you know, a piece of Lester came off right in my hands in front of her. I was red as a lobster, the heat from my face outdoing the summer sun. But she got a kick out of it, laughing like it was the funniest thing she'd ever seen. And somehow, that laughter made me feel less like a fool and more like I might just be able to pull this whole "charming the girl" thing off. We ended up sharing a basket of fried clams and holding hands under the boardwalk that night, the warmth of her touch sending a jolt of happiness straight through me. It felt like the ocean had orchestrated the whole thing, just another one of her little gifts for me.

Those early days at the beach laid the foundation for my becoming a man. The ocean was my first real love, and like any infatuated teenager, I shaped my whole life around chasing her, and being close to her. Everything else paled in comparison to the constant pull of the tides, the hum of the waves in the back of my mind. I picked my jobs, my friends, and my hangouts, all based on proximity to the good old Atlantic. Everything revolved around her in some way, even if I didn't realize it at the time. She was mostly all I ever wanted to talk about, think about, and dream about. Whether it was the endless horizon that made me feel small and free at the same time, or the rhythm of the waves crashing against the shore that seemed to speak directly to my soul, she consumed my thoughts. The ocean was both my escape and my anchor, the place where I could lose myself and, at the same time, find who I truly was.

More than that, the skills I picked up letting the ocean slap me around and teach me her secrets set me up for everything that came next. he patience I learned waiting on a big swell, watching the water shift and roll, knowing that good things come to those who wait, whether it's a perfect wave or the right moment in life has been invaluable. The stamina from fighting a 20-pound striper on the line, the instincts I honed navigating through pea soup fog to find safe harbor all added up to a keen sense of how to read the tides, literal and figurative. It became clear to me that life, just like the ocean, is unpredictable. Sometimes calm and serene, other times wild and unforgiving. But the trick is to ride both with the same resolve. Running a business, hell, running a family takes the same balance of surrender and grit, nose-down hurricane riding, and sun-warmed floating I first found in the sea. The same ebb and flow, the same give and take. No matter how much time passes, the rhythm of life never really changes.

These days, my dance steps are a little slower, my bare feet dig a little deeper in the wet sand. But the wonder is still there. Old salts like me, our hearts never age, not if we can still feel that first tug of the tide, that first tickle of foam on the ankles that set us off on a lifetime of watery devotion. I'll never stop letting her toss me around and teach me, never lose the little kid's giddiness of watching her dancing waves. And if once in a while, a pretty little starfish catches my eye, well, it won't bother the missus. She knows I'm a one-ocean man.

Homemade "windows" for catching scallops. Hang over the side of a drifting skiff, look through the glass at the bottom.

Sunrise over Narragansett Beach

CHAPTER 3:
LIFEGUARD DAYS

Picture this: it's the summer of 1979, and I'm 18 years old, bronzed and buff from spending every waking minute at the beach. I'm perched high up in my lifeguard chair, red buoy at my feet, zinc oxide on my nose, surveying my kingdom of sand and sea. To my left and right, the Rhode Island shore stretches out like a promise, dotted with oiled bodies glistening in the sun, each one basking in the warmth, their carefree laughter mixing with the sound of crashing waves. The salt air kisses my cheeks as I squint into the glare, scanning the horizon for any signs of trouble. I'd waited my whole adolescence for this moment, to officially be one of those guardians of the coast I'd idolized since I was a lanky kid getting worked by the shore break. Now here I was, Lord of the Beach, master of all I surveyed, feeling the wind in my hair and the sun on my face, every inch of me filled with pride. And getting paid to do it, no less! For an ocean-obsessed teenager, landing that first lifeguarding gig at Narragansett Beach was like hitting the jackpot. I couldn't believe they were going to give me money to sit around and stare at the water all day, maybe pluck a few damsels in distress out of the drink occasionally. Little did I know how much actual work was involved in keeping watch over those rolling aquamarine playgrounds. Guarding wasn't a job for the faint of heart or for the weakness of biceps. We had to re-certify every spring and prove we had the endurance and strength to haul drowning victims to safety in even the roughest conditions. The training was grueling, but nothing beats the rush of saving someone or knowing that I was standing between the ocean and those who might get caught in her depths. By the time I was in my early 20s, I was a senior staff member, and my buddies and I did not like doing the swim tests after so many years of proving ourselves. We were seasoned, and it felt a little ridiculous to have to prove something we'd already demonstrated a hundred times over in real life. Fortunately, the State didn't pay much attention to us senior staffers, and there were no computers to verify information, so we usually paid a few rookies we trusted to take the pool test. Those kinds of things were easy to get away with in the 80s. The State was none the wiser, and the newbies were eager to help because they thought it would earn them special treatment on the beaches. They took our money, then after they'd passed their tests for themselves, they'd sign in with our names, and we'd all get a little check that meant we could continue our positions as lifeguards. It felt like a rite of passage in a way, something that everyone did to keep the gears of the beach running smoothly. I don't feel bad about it because I never put anyone's life in danger. I'm a strong swimmer, but I'm not a fast swimmer. Still never stopped me from performing dozens of rescues over the five years I spent in the tower. Each one was a reminder of just how unpredictable the ocean could be, and how lucky I was to be part of a team that kept her mysteries in check.

The surf test was a completely different beast. You'd be shocked how many buff gym-rat pretty boys crumbled like a sandcastle at high tide when you put them in open water. It was a whole other beast; those guys might look strong on land, but once they were out there in the ocean, all that muscle didn't count for much when the waves were crashing and the water was cold. To pass the test, you must swim for a quarter mile, row the skiff, and paddle out the paddle boards, performing actual rescues on dummies in the surf—some singles and sometimes with a towline. That was a real demonstration of bravado. I loved showing off for the rookies and the other beaches; I'd paddle the 12-foot rescue board, row a lifeboat, and run for miles to stay in shape. It wasn't just about the physical grind, there was a rhythm to it, more like a dance with the ocean. You had to trust your instincts and experience, and sometimes just throw caution to the wind. And when you nailed it, when you made a perfect rescue or came in on that final wave after a grueling workout, the sense of accomplishment was like nothing else. You felt like you were part of something bigger than yourself, part of the sea and the coast you were guarding. It wasn't just a job; it was a way of life.

The secret to being a good guard was never taking your eyes off the waves. Most folks picture lifeguarding as eight hours of tanning and flexing in between flirting and rubbing baby oil on babes, but the reality was a hell of a lot more intense, especially on days with large surf. It wasn't all fun and games, those big days were when the real work happened. There could be 10 or more rescues on a day when the surf swelled to six or eight feet. People love to play in the waves when they're like that, coming to the beach in droves with friends and family to frolic in nature's aquatic playground, but very few can handle the powerful ocean water over their hips. It pounds them into the sand or pulls them out 100 yards in minutes, often without warning, as if the sea had a mind that could change at any moment. The ocean was unpredictable—one minute, calm and inviting, the next, it could turn into a furious beast, pulling anyone too careless into its depths. We had to keep an eye on the water all the time, feeling the pulse of the waves, anticipating the changes in their rhythm, and always aware of how quickly things could turn dangerous. A summer on guard consists of taking care of broken bones, sunstroke, bee stings, skin cuts, and avoiding vomiting beachgoers. It's a far cry from the carefree days people imagine, but it was a responsibility I never took lightly. The ocean is beautiful but also relentless, and as a lifeguard, you stand between that beauty and its sometimes-deadly force. But the heart of it all was the rescues—I was always good at the rescues; that's where being a strong swimmer helps. We would take turns at the first aid area, and I could handle the bleeding, broken bones—even the compound fractures where the bone had pierced through the skin, although fire and rescue would be called for those injuries that required more than a bandage. There was only one thing that always bothered me and still does—the smell of vomit. Whenever I encountered it on the job, I would sometimes join the kid on the bucket or run to the sand on the side of the building. These were not my finest moments, but we all have our weaknesses. The ocean, in all its glory and fury, had a way of reminding us of our own limitations. On the heavy surf days, time flew so fast that I never got a glimpse of the bikini-clad, oiled-up goddesses. When I was up in that tower, my focus never wavered. I scanned the beach with the intensity and precision of a hawk hunting prey. Distraction meant death in this line of work—one moment of lost attention could mean a life lost. The ocean was unforgiving, and my job was to stand guard against it, to respect its power while still serving as a protector. Still today, I scan the water like a hawk, only now it's for other boaters, or obstacles such as rocks. I never take my eyes off the water.

After watching and waiting, I got pretty damn good at reading the signs of a swimmer in distress. You'd think it would be all arms waving and "Help, I'm drowning!" like you see in the movies. But nine times out of 10, it was way more subtle than that. The ocean, with its relentless push and pull, has a way of concealing danger until it is nearly too late. Usually, there was just a look of wide-eyed panic on their face, a slight desperation in their movements. They'd be fighting to keep their chin above the foam, taking in water every time they opened their mouth to shout, their bodies caught in the undertow, the saltwater stinging their eyes and blurring their vision. The waves, often unmerciful, seemed to play with them, dragging them under only to throw them back up again, just enough to make them gasp for air before pulling them back into the depths. If you tuned out for even a second, and stopped your constant visual sweep, you might miss it, and then you'd have a body on your hands. The ocean is meant to be understood only. She does not care if you were paying attention or not—it's a force of nature, indifferent to human struggle, and that's why you had to be constantly alert, your senses attuned to every slight movement in the water, every shift in the tide.

On average, I probably made a rescue every seven to 10 days. But during peak season, I was plucking hapless tourists out of riptides daily. They had no idea what they were up against, blissfully unaware of the raw power of the ocean they were diving into. The ocean is beautiful, captivating even, but it has no mercy when it comes to those who take it for granted. They'd get caught in a rip and suddenly find themselves being dragged out to the open ocean faster than they could say Marco Polo. That's when the freak-outs happened—flailing arms, kicking legs, big lungfuls of brine, and sheer terror. In those moments, the ocean was a blur of motion and sound, waves crashing, water rushing, and all the while, I had to stay calm, focused, and ready. It was a battle between fear and the instinct to survive, and every time someone got caught in that riptide, the fight against the ocean was as real as it could get.

I won't lie; there were times when a rescue got dicey. When a grown man is seeing his life flash before his eyes, when he feels that black abyss reaching up to claim him, he'll do anything to keep from going under. I can't tell you how many times some beefy dude tried to climb me like a ladder, desperate to get a gulp of air. Never mind that I'm there to save him, in his lizard brain, I'm just a buoy he needs to cling to. In those moments, the ocean becomes a ruthless force, and sometimes, the human instinct to survive can turn dangerous for everyone involved. That's when a guard must get mean. When some 200-pound slab of panicked humanity is trying to push you under to save himself, you can't mess around. The sea doesn't care if you're trying to save a life—if you can't assert control over the situation, you're both in trouble. More than once, I had to give a fighting victim a sharp elbow to the solar plexus or a good hard jab to the nose just to stun him long enough to break his death grip on my torso. A casual observer might have thought I was trying to drown the poor slob, what with all the dunking and shoving. But it was either assert dominance fast or risk us both ending up as crab food on the bottom. In those moments, the ocean was a tug-of-war between life and death, a battle of strength and survival. Once I established who the rescuer and rescuee were, I'd lock my arm around their chest and sidestroke us back to the beach. There were a few dicey moments over the years, but by the grace of Poseidon, I never lost a victim.

Rescues weren't always so dramatic, though. For every amped-up wrestler trying to suplex me into the undertow, a dozen little kids drifted out a bit too far, chasing minnows. The vast and ever-moving ocean could swallow them up without a second thought, but their innocence and trust in me made my job a little easier. I'd see that little glimmer of fear in their eyes, the sudden realization that their feet couldn't touch bottom anymore and the beach seemed far away suddenly. The ocean, which had once seemed so playful and inviting, was now a daunting force. Some would just freeze up, too scared to even dog paddle. Others would start wailing for their moms like they were auditioning for the Titanic sequel. Those were the easy ones. I'd just cruise out there on my board, flash a big grin, scoop them up, and deliver them back to a hysterical parent or nanny. The kids were always stoked; they thought I was some kind of superhero for fishing them out of the deep end. The moms tended to get a bit handsy in their gratitude, if you catch my drift. Let's just say there's a reason lifeguards are always rocking those mirrored shades. Of course, some rescues were less adorable and more... unsanitary. I can't count how many "Code Vomits" I've handled, how many half-digested hot dogs and Cheetos I've watched float by while dragging some seasick landlubber back to shore. The rookies always lost their own lunch the first time they got barfed on during a rescue. You must have a stomach of steel in this gig, along with the biceps. Diarrhea and ocean water is a gnarly combo, trust me on that one.

Then there were the injuries. The fact that people will just let their kids race into the surf without a thought to what's beneath the surface never ceases to amaze me. The shore is as beautiful and inviting as it is dangerous, and it's a shame how often people forget the risks lurking just beneath the surface. I popped enough urchin spines out of tender feet and pried enough fishhooks out of hands and legs to last a lifetime. Every time I pulled another barb out of someone's skin, I felt that familiar surge of frustration—frustration that people don't realize the power of the sea and don't always respect what lies beneath the calm waters. One of my worst was this poor kid, probably all of six years old, just minding his business building a sandcastle when some numb-nut tourist tried to cast right over his head. Got the tyke's ear instead. I was picking bits of seaworm guts and barbs out of his earlobe for an hour while he screamed bloody murder. I could feel the weight of every agonized scream and knew that, once again, the beach had turned from a playground to a battlefield, with the ocean playing the role of an unforgiving foe.

Worst of all were the spinal injuries. Every guard's nightmare is seeing some hotshot daredevil sprint down the beach, launch himself into a shallow breaker, and just... not get back up. The ocean's beauty can turn deadly in an instant, especially when it hides rocks or sandbars just beneath the surface. It's an awful sight—the way the body crumples, the stillness that follows as the waves continue rolling in, indifferent. The whole beach goes silent, holding its breath, while you're racing through the foam, praying it's not as bad as you know it is. Those few seconds, between seeing the injury and assessing whether it's a break or just a jolt, felt like hours. Usually they're just a bit stunned, the wind knocked out of them, but man, those few seconds before they start moving again are the longest of your life. I've been lucky—never had a paralysis on my watch, but the fear of it, the weight of that responsibility, always hovered over me, the unseen presence that kept my vigilance sharp. The ocean demands respect, and sometimes, it tests that respect in the most terrifying ways.

It gives me chills just thinking about it. People don't realize how dangerous something as innocent-seeming as body surfing can be. The ocean's not a theme park, as much as we try to make it one. There's no net at the bottom, no safety shut-off. When Mama Ocean has a mood swing, all you can do is respect her and try to stay out of her way.

Guarding took more than muscles and first aid training, though. You had to have a way with people, an instinct for crowd control, and keeping the peace. When you jammed that many hot, half-naked bodies in a small stretch of sand, things were bound to get a bit wild. The sea was unpredictable, but so were the people who came to enjoy it—beachgoers brought their own storms, usually in the form of tempers. Tempers would flare over everything from who got to claim the best patch of shade to whose boom box was blaring the loudest, as if the music itself could drown out the sound of the waves. It was up to us to make sure those little spats didn't turn into a full-on beach blanket brawl.

I learned quickly that a light touch and a joke would get you a lot further in those situations than flexing authority. People didn't want to feel like they were being lectured or bossed around—they just wanted to enjoy the beach. You just sidle up to the aggro Speedo-wearer or outraged Frisbee-thrower, flash that megawatt smile, and make some crack about how the only thing that should be getting heated around here is the suntan oil. You'd catch them off guard, easing the tension without even trying. Maybe throw in a line about how there's enough sand for everyone, we're all just here to have a good time—99% of the time, that charm offensive would do the trick, and I could get back to the serious business of achieving the perfect all-over bronzing. You learn when to fight when to let things roll, and when to bring people back to earth with a well-timed joke.

Not that it was all glamorous, mind you. For every hero moment plucking a flailing kid from the jaws of the salty deep, there were hours of tedium. The ocean might give you those heart-pounding rescues, but the rest of the time, it tested your endurance in other ways—like the blazing sun. The sun could be brutal at midday, just pounding down on you from that big, cloudless sky. The relentless heat from the overhead sun would bake you in your little wooden tower, turning the air into something thick and suffocating. The ocean had its power, but the sun was no less fierce in its own way. Baking in your little wooden tower, you'd start to go a bit loopy. I used to dream of giant umbrellas, or at least one of those little travel fans the old ladies were always using to cool their faces.

And sweet baby Jesus on a surfboard, the boredom. People think it must be so exciting, getting paid to sit on the beach all day, but let me tell you, when the waves are flat and the crowd is sparse, the minutes crawl by like slugs through molasses. There's only so much flexing and whistling you can do before you start to get existential. You find yourself pondering life's big questions, like how that one seagull always seems to know when someone's about to toss a crust and what exactly is in a Cheese Doodle anyway?

But then a set would roll in, the beach would pop off with hoots of laughter and shrieks of watery glee, and just like that, my excitement was back. Any shred of ennui or mundanity would vanish like sea foam on the breeze. The sea has a way of drawing you in, of resetting everything with its rhythmic waves and endless beauty. Any shred of ennui or mundanity would vanish like sea foam on the breeze, swallowed by the pulse of the sea. The smile would creep back, and

I'd lean into the weight of the sun on my shoulders, the sticky sea air prickling my nose and the delicious soreness of overused muscles as I settled in for another eight hours of doing what I loved. It was as if the ocean itself was reminding me why I was there and had chosen this path—immersed in nature, in something so wild and free. Because in the end, there was still no better job on Earth for all the baggage that came with the gig—the vomit and the sunburn and the chafed inner thighs. To spend every day in communion with the ocean, a first-hand witness to all her many moods and mysteries. To make my living by plunging headfirst into the churning blue soup, feeling the roar and pulse of a force so much bigger and more timeless than my little human self. There was a humbling truth in knowing that you were part of something that had been there long before you and would continue on long after. To be a part of people's beach days, their sandy childhood memories, and splashy moments of pure uncut joy. Yeah, it was worth a bit of monotony now and then. The quiet moments, the slow lulls between the action, were just the backdrop to everything that truly mattered—the ocean, the people, and the freedom of everything. To this day, you can hardly drag me out of the water. The call of the sea, that relentless pull, is something that never fades. And hey, it didn't hurt that there was an endless supply of tanned female flesh to admire, a constant parade of itty-bitty bikinis just begging for some lifeguard love. But that's a whole other set of stories that you're gonna have to buy me a drink or three to unlock, and I don't drink anymore. Suffice it to say, my after-hours exploits could fill a book twice as long as this one.

For now, I'll tell you one of the tales of a night spent devoted to debauchery, although I'll leave out the debauchery bits. Use your imagination. When I was a young buck of 17, two of my buddies were sleeping over so we could sneak out in the middle of the night and go to a beach party. We slowly and quietly opened the manual garage door, wincing every time it creaked in complaint. Once the door was up, one of us steered, and the other pushed the car out of the garage, down the driveway, and into the street before we dared to crank the engine. Boy, there was something exhilarating about sneaking around in the dark, the thrill of the moment blending with the salty night air. The bonfire was already raging by the time we made it two miles down the street to the beach. We had a grand old time, then when it was time to go home, we reversed our steps–driving until we were about a block away from my house, then turning off the engine and pushing the car back into the garage. The quietness of those final moments, sneaking back into the garage like nothing ever happened, felt like a small rebellion against the world outside. After meticulously pulling the garage door closed again, we went to bed with satisfied grins. The orchestration was smooth. Flawless. Or so we thought. The following morning, as my mother made pancakes for three hungry boys, my father sauntered into the kitchen and sat down at the table with us.

"Have fun last night?" he asked us.

My friends and I locked eyes. We thought we were in the clear. "What do you mean, Dad?" I asked, playing dumb.

My dad looked down his nose at me. "I never would have known, but I backed the car in last night, and now it's facing forward."

He wasn't even angry, though; he was impressed. I'd gotten away with my shenanigans and was rewarded with all the pancakes I could eat. Life was good.

Those years on the stand shaped me as a man. They taught me that life, like the ocean, is a force to be reckoned with, respected, and never underestimated. The ocean has a way of humbling you, of reminding you that no matter how strong or prepared you think you are, there's always something bigger and more powerful lurking beneath the surface. That real toughness is quiet, steady under pressure and always keeping a watchful eye out for those not strong enough to help themselves. That you take your fun where you can get it, because you never know when the tides are going to turn. And the very best things in life—a perfect bluebird beach day, a nubile California blonde with mischief in her eyes, the sweet spot on a wave where everything goes weightless and sparkly for a Magic stretch—are always worth diving deep for.

A group of the lifeguards. That's me in the upper left with a mop of dark hair. Those were great days.

Me rowing the beach dory to stay in shape. I rowed four miles every couple of days.

Me paddling the rescue board a few miles every few days—
sometimes even surfed it into the beach

CHAPTER 4:
THE PARTY ISLAND

Block Island. Just saying the name out loud brings a rush of salt air and cheap beer to my senses, a swirling kaleidoscope of sunburned bodies and neon biker shorts, of thumping sound systems and shrieking gulls and the endless, glorious possibilities contained in a seemingly bottomless cup of jungle juice. If you were a New England kid in the '80s and '90s and you liked to party, you knew the beacon of hedonism that was good old Block Island. It was our Promised Land, a brackish Shangri-La where the alcohol flowed like seawater, and the dress code usually started with "optional." My love affair with that raucous little paradise started the same way most of my youthful fancies did—with a bikini and a bad idea. Picture: 1981. I'm 19, lifeguarding during the day, and at night, I'm bartending in Narragansett, slinging drinks at this beachside watering hole, a joint so divey, you practically had to be up to date on your tetanus shot just to sit on the barstools. In walks these two drop-dead gorgeous beach bunnies, all tan lines and Coppertone, the kind of girls who make a red-blooded man forget he's supposed to be tending the bar. They sidle up to my well-worn patch of mahogany and order something frilly, like a pair of Bay Breezes or Sex on The Beaches, I can't remember.

What I do remember is the way the conversation sparked and crackled like driftwood catching a match to gasoline. Before I knew it, we were swapping stories and double entendres, the early evening crowd of salty fishermen and leathery barflies fading into so much background noise. By the end of my shift, I felt like I'd known these chicks forever, or at least long enough to make what was no doubt a very foolhardy proposal.

"Hey, I've got tomorrow off and was thinking about boating over to Block Island for the day. Any chance you ladies would want to come along? I could use a couple of first mates to help me navigate if you catch my drift..."

They caught it alright, as evidenced by the giggles, the hair twirling, and the exaggerated lip biting that commenced to transpire. Quicker than you could say, "anchors aweigh," Operation What Could Possibly Go Wrong was in full effect. Now, I know what you're thinking. "But Ron, you salty sea dog, you surely a man of your nautical prowess and island hopping experiences, had been to Block Island a million times at that point, right?" Wrong, my friend. As I bobbed fitfully in my bunk that night, visions of shipwrecks and Coast Guard rescues dancing in my head, and the cold reality began to sink in. I, Ronald Smith, had just committed to piloting a pair of nubile strangers across 12 miles of open ocean to New

England's most notorious lush playground… having never made the crossing myself.

But fortune favors the bold and the slightly insane, or so I've always told myself. As the morning sun appeared and I fired up my trusty 21-foot boat, I swear I could hear a wispy voice on the breeze whispering, "Send it, Ronnie boy. Full speed ahead and damn the torpedoes." To the girls' credit, they showed up right on time--I'm a stickler for punctuality-wearing fantastic bikinis. The next thing I remember, we were skipping across the West Gap like a stone on a mill pond, my new friends' blond hair whipping in the wind as they whooped with beer-soaked glee. The 12-mile crossing itself is a bit of a blur, a frothy mélange of flying spray and fluttering bikini straps that resolved into high-def focus the second what looked like land came into view. All I remember clearly is the sea was calm, and the sun was shining. There she was—Block Island, shimmering on the horizon like a green flash at sunset. I felt my pulse quicken as we drew closer, the rocky bluffs and pristine beaches resolving into a postcard-perfect vision of maritime nirvana. All at once, I was struck by the irrational certainty that something monumental was about to happen, that stepping onto those sandy shores was going to change my life in ways I couldn't yet imagine. Although I'd lived only 12 miles from it for so long, I had never yet been and knew I would no longer be the same man once my feet touched the sandy shores of the infamous party island. Of course, I had to get us there in one piece before any life-altering could commence. Drawing closer to the island, I had a choice to make: left or right. I didn't have a clue, but I figured it was an island. If I went the wrong way, I could just circle around until I found the beach. Fortunately, I guessed correctly on my first try–it was left, which boosted my confidence. Eureka! The harbor came into view. There could not be a more perfect Saturday.

As the breakwaters of Old Harbor loomed before me, I realized with a sinking feeling that I hadn't the foggiest idea how to negotiate the boat traffic and tricky currents to land this tub safely. But if there's one thing I learned in my guarding days, it's that there's no better camouflage than confidence. Act like you belong, and nine times out of ten, people will believe you do.

So, I puffed out my chest, affected an expression of seasoned nonchalance, and glided past the rock opening like I'd been parking boats since the days of whaling barks and peg legs. I hooked the stern anchor on the beach on the first toss, and the bow in the water was close enough with the other boats and the beach, and I'll give myself credit for doing a halfway decent job of it, because the next thing I knew, we were tied up snug as bugs in rugs, not a stitch of fiberglass out of place. As I helped my new lady friends onto the beach with what I hoped was a rakish twinkle in my eye, I felt a surge of cocky invincibility. Damn, maybe this salty captain schtick really suited me! They kept remarking on how safe they felt in my skilled hands, and using these skilled hands; I ended up dating both briefly. But any delusions of Horatio Hornblower grandeur were quickly eclipsed by the electric thrill of last stepping onto that fabled isle. From the second my flipflops hit the weathered planks of the harborside promenade, I could feel that inimitable Block Island vibe, that giddy tingle of sunstruck revelry and hushed debauchery that seemed to shimmer in the salty air like a mirage. Everywhere I looked were bleary-eyed beauties and raucous bands of seagoing miscreants, all of them hell-bent on wringing every ounce of excitement from this gray-shingle Xanadu.

And oh, the bars. Dear reader, if I live to be a hundred and twenty, I'll never forget my first glimpse inside Captain Nick's and The National. The way they seemed to stretch on forever in the gin-soaked afternoon light, an endless human tangle of slurring lips and roaming hands and spilled Heineken that resolved into a single undulating organism. I felt like Darwin stumbling onto the Galapagos, my mind reeling with the staggering diversity of hook-up hunting fauna on display.

Within minutes, we were swept up in the boozy bacchanalia, ricocheting from tap to tap and toast to sloppy toast. My new friends seemed to know the moves to this debauched dance by heart, shimmying their way through the beer-stained labyrinth like a pair of homing pigeons zeroing in on the nearest frat basement. I followed in their wake, slurping from proffered Solo cups and adding my voice to the Dionysian din. Like the festivities of the ancient Greeks and Romans, the environment was rife with intoxicants and void of inhibitions. As the afternoon wore on and the edges of sobriety blurred beyond recognition, I began to pick up on my fellow revelers' strange, unspoken customs. There was an odd sort of decorum to their giddy nihilism, a tipsy code of conduct more sway than stricture. It was all winks and good-natured elbow jabs, a "you dump your drink on me, I dump mine on you" school of roughhousing bonhomie that felt vaguely feral and undeniably arousing.

After what could have been hours or eons, we spilled back out into the sultry island twilight, the three of us propping each other up like the world's most dysfunctional tent poles. As the first stars pricked the indigo sky and the beery numbness slowly gave way to a second (or was it third?) wind, I found myself steering our little convoy towards the soft lap of the darkened shore.

At that time, this was one of the longest trips I had ever taken, and I was blinded by the blackness of the night and a light fog. Without GPS (only the government had it back then), I relied on my trusty compass, chart, and depth finder. Setting a course for the mainland, I went slow like a pro. While I couldn't see much, I got us there safely, and most importantly, the girls thought they were in such safe hands with an experienced captain.

What happened next is probably best left to the feverish imaginings of my gentler readers and the fond, fuzzy memories of this lifeguard extraordinaire. Let's just say that the waves weren't the only things crashing that night, nor the surf, the only salty tumult erupting in the peachy afterglow of a Block Island sunset. As I drifted off to sleep on the gently pitching deck of my stalwart vessel sometime before the roosters stirred, I thought to myself, "Buddy, you may have just found your second home."

And oh, what a home it was. That inaugural crossing may have been the first, but it was far from the last. Over the next few summers, I returned to the Brigadoon of the Boat Set every chance I got, each time lured by the siren song of rollicking nights and Cuervo-clouded days. The island became my own Bermuda Triangle, a place where hours disappeared and brain cells went to die, but man, oh man, what a way to go.

Not all my outings to the island were laced with debauchery. Once, my mother's brother came for a visit, and my mother thought it would be nice to take Uncle Chuck to Block Island for some sightseeing and lunch. At this point, I knew how to navigate straight to the harbor and anchor there with the bow in the deep water and the stern against the beach, like a clothesline. After parking like a pro, we made our way to The National for lunch. We sat down at our outdoor table on the porch and ordered. It was a gorgeous day, so I basked in the beauty of the passersby, ignoring many loud blasts of ferry horns until my eyes inevitably traced back to the harbor. This is a federal dockage area, and the main user is a ferry line. Those ferries were 150 to 250-foot steel ships that needed a wide berth, and there in the middle of the passageway was my little 22-foot boat, holding up traffic. The bow anchor held strong, but the stern anchor had come loose, so my boat was swinging around in the middle of the channel while the ferries wailed on their horns and steered around the obstacle some idiot (me) had left in their path. I tore down the beach, all the while questioning how I was going to fix my problem. I'm a strong swimmer, but I needed to swim 200 feet, start the engine, and back the boat away from the channel without tangling the bowline under the boat.

Not knowing what else to do, I swam to the boat as fast as I could with the stern anchor and the line in one hand, placed them on the platform, climbed into the boat, and leaped to the driver's seat. Since most boaters are honest, the key was already in the ignition, so I started her up and guided her back to her position on the clothesline. Then, after re-anchoring, I went back to finish my lunch.

My Uncle Chuck passed away in 2005, but he didn't miss an opportunity to bust my balls about that mishap until the day he died. I miss that guy and'll never forget that day on Block Island in Old Harbor. I also have many fond memories of New Harbor, which is the State-run side and very monied. The party atmosphere is more sophisticated over there, and the boats are much fancier. I used to go out with a huge group of friends, all rafted together. This was the social event of the summer with grilling, drinking, and all the water toys you can imagine–floats, rafts, paddleboards. The drinking started around noon and lasted well into the night. Once the moon came out, the shenanigans began.

On more than one occasion, I got lost in the dinghy with friends while returning to the boat from shore at midnight. In the pouring rain, with the blinding white lights of 500 others shining in our faces, never mind the fog. It wasn't upsetting, though; it was hilarious, even when finding our boat took over an hour. There are a lot of activities available at New Harbor, so we would also make day trips to other beaches and visit friends. On one of those outings, I foolishly brought my Rolex instead of my Dive watch, placing it in the Velcro pocket of our soft cooler. After a long day at the beach with 20 to 30 of my closest friends, we started packing the dinghies for the mile-long journey back to the boats. Everything was covered in sand, so I dumped the cooler out right before I remembered the watch.

"Oh, shit!" I cried. But it was too late. The Rolex hit her watery grave with a kerplunk that haunts me to this day. I recruited seven friends to put on fins and masks, and we dove, searching the area for hours. The muddy bottom made it impossible to find anything, so although I was heartbroken, we had to give up. The Block Island giveth, and the Block Island taketh. It's a small price to pay after all she's done for me.

With each trip to the island, I fell a little more in love with Bacchus's own zip code, where the wine and revelry flowed freely. The heady perfume of low tide mingled with the yeasty whiff of the breakfast crowds at Rachael's (now called Ellen's). The way the noon sun would pound the cobblestones of Water Street until the whole place shimmered like some feverish mirage, a wobbly Sahara by the sea full of bleached hair and baked skin.

By night, the Gomorrah vibes only intensified. The thump-thump of sound systems rattled windowpanes and eardrums alike. The sticky film of spilled margaritas glazing dance floors and inhibitions. The way stoplights would melt into rosy smears in the twilight, and everything got soft around the edges, all Vaseline on the lens and puckered flesh in the shadows.

There was this one bar in particular, The Yellow Kitten, that always seemed to be the eye of the hurricane. It was like a giant petri dish of party fouls and pheromones. You could practically feel the barn-burning energy crackling off the queue of tank tops and popped collars snaking out the door. Inside, the writhing mass of sweaty, over-served creatures only paused its bacchanalian churning for the 10 seconds it took to screech along with the ubiquitous opening riffs of "Sweet Home Alabama."

I spent more lump dawns than I care to recall stumbling out of that godforsaken paradise, my ears ringing and my shirt stuck to my back from some goon's upturned Pabst. Sometimes, I'd be arm-in-arm with a bikini-clad partner in crime, her flip-flops dangling from one hand as she giggled at the joke of a line I'd managed to slur out between hiccups. Other times I'd be propping up a buddy like a frat house maypole, both of us seeing double from whatever well tequila and Tang concoction they'd been ladling out in Dixie cups. But no matter how pickled or plastered I got, I always made sure to be down by the docks in time to catch the first glimpse of the morning ferries pulling out of port. There was something about watching those great big beasts back out into open water that just set my synapses to singing, even on five hours of comatose sleep and enough Cuervo to embalm a small platoon. As I'd watch the bleary-eyed, Mardi-Grasbead-strewn revelers squint against the piercing sunshine, I'd feel a twinge of something like pride. "That's right, amateurs," I'd chuckle to myself. "This is how the pros play."

Because that's what we were—professional funologists, summa cum laude from the school of hard knocks and last calls. While the weekend warriors were nursing their hangovers on the slow boat back to real life, my sandy tribe was already peeling off last night's beer koozies and cracking open a breakfast Bud. For us, the party never stopped. It just relocated from the bar to the beach and back again in an endless loop of sun-dappled dissolution.

You see, that was the secret to living the Block Island dream—total commitment to the bit. You had to lean all the way in, let the dizzy swirl of sand and skin and bottom-shelf liquor seep down into your marrow until you forgot there was any other way to be. Only then could you truly understand the magic of that fuzzy place between the lost and the found, where every sunrise was a blank slate and every bonfire a Viking funeral for the person you used to be.

It was a pace and a place that didn't lend itself to longevity, at least not of the spiritual sort. But damn if it didn't make a body feel alive while it lasted. Coursing with cut-rate hooch and zinging with the reckless energy of untested youth, we'd howl at that big butter moon like a pack of juiced-up coyotes, hungry and unstoppable.

Of course, even the wildest rumpuses must take a knee at some point. As the summers went by and the hangovers got a little harder to shake, nature forced me to slow down. My trips to the foggy, boggy Eden at the edge of the sound tapered off, the glitter of the can blizzards dulling just a touch as the leaves began to turn.

But to this day, I'll catch a whiff of Coppertone mixing with a low-hanging cloud of Marlboro Reds, and boom, I'm right back there. Sticky with Mad Dog and bad decisions, dancing on a picnic table like it's my own private soapbox. Those Block Island nights stay with you, long after the last ferry has chugged out of port and the puke has been hosed off the promenade.

So, here's to you, my sweet little hot mess of an aisle. You taught this crusty old sea dog some of life's most important lessons - that tequila is not a breakfast food, the sea is the best hangover cure, that you should always carry bail money in your clothes, and that you can never wear enough sunscreen when afternoon delight is on the docket. Most of all, you showed me what it means to really let go, to cannonball into the deep end of now, and let the riptides take you where they may.

Block Island, I salute you. You crazy, booze-soaked, heart-capturing SOB, here's to the memories, however hazy and hungover they may be. Stay salty, my friends.

The Great Salt Pond (New Harbor), Block Island. Easily over 1000 boats among docks, mooring balls, and free anchorage.

Rafting in New Harbor. The toys and alcohol flowed freely. Friends we met were the best; many are friends to this day

The National Hotel overlooking Old Harbor—the front porch was the best place to be in daytime.

CHAPTER 5:
FISH TALES

There's something about being out on the open water, just you and the vast blue expanse, that strips away all the bullshit and noise of everyday life. No boss breathing down your neck, no bills piling up on the counter, no ladyfolk busting your balls about forgetting to put the toilet seat down again. Out there, it's just you versus your wits versus whatever finned Leviathan happens to be cruising the depths that day. And for me, that elemental contest of hunter and hunted is about as pure as existence gets, a refreshing escape that feels almost primordial.

I've been chasing scaly tails since I was old enough to hold a Zebco, but it wasn't until my late teens that I really started to appreciate the art and science of angling. Maybe it was all those long, golden hours I spent perched in a lifeguard chair, studying the rhythms and moods of the ocean as it ebbed and flowed like some giant, breathing organism. Or perhaps it was just the natural progression of a water-obsessed kid, captivated by the symphony of splashes and sun-kissed waves, looking for new ways to commune with his first love. Either way, by the time I hit my 20s, I was fully hooked (pun most definitely intended) on the thrill of the fight and the chase— the intoxicating dance of predator and prey that becomes an almost spiritual pursuit.

Now, when most folks think of fishing, they picture some grizzled old coot snoozing in a folding chair, a straw hat tipped over his eyes, and a line dangling listlessly in some muddy creek. But let me tell you, the kind of fishing that lit my fire was about as far from that sleepy stereotype as you can get. I was all about the big game, the mean marine machines that could strip a reel and snap a rod like a toothpick if you didn't know what the hell you were doing. Every trip out on the ocean felt like stepping into a new chapter of an exhilarating adventure novel, with every cast an open invitation to the unknown.

Sharks and tuna—those were my poisons of choice. I loved the raw power of those alpha predators, the way they could explode out of the depths like a torpedo and dance across the surface like some kind of demented aquatic ballerina. Hooking into one of those bad boys was like lassoing a thunderbolt—all furious energy and electric jolts shot straight up the braided line, coursing through my very being. Each encounter sent a rush of adrenaline through me, flooding my system with the purest effervescence of being alive. Fishing the canyons with Mike and Chad Burr was always an adventure that felt more like a high-speed chase with nature—

except the chase was happening in the middle of the ocean, 100 miles offshore. They were a father-son duo who had the soul of pirates, but without all the pillaging. Just the love of the sea— and the fish. We'd head out to the deep canyons, a place where the sea floor drops from a modest 300 feet to a jaw-dropping 2000 feet. It's like the ocean decided, "You want tuna? Fine, but you're going to have to earn it."

Tuna don't hang out near the coast like some kind of lazy beach bum—they prefer the warmer waters out in the canyons, where the Gulf Stream delivers a tropical heatwave, and the air is 20 degrees warmer than back on the mainland. It's like they all got an invite to a secret oceanic party, and we're just trying to crash it. The whole area is a feeding frenzy —yellowfin, bluefin, bigeye, and albacore are all there, indulging in the buffet brought up by the upswell. Picture thousands of pounds of bait fish doing an involuntary bungee jump from the ocean floor to the surface, and all the big predators are there to scoop up the feast. It's the oceanic version of a 24-hour all-you-can-eat sushi bar, and the tunas are VIPs.

But the real oddball in this warm water buffet is the Mahi Mahi. These fish don't care about water temperature like the rest of the cool crowd. They could be 50 miles offshore, all the way into the canyon. Great eating fish, and their reproductive speed is straight-up freaky—they go from newborn to three feet long in less than a year! So, if you hook a four-to-five-foot bull, you're dealing with a true veteran of the deep. Meanwhile, there are other creatures lurking about, like bottlenose dolphins, common dolphins, and even whales, all eating their fill. The place is alive—like the ocean's version of a wild buffet restaurant, where everyone's trying to get their share before it closes.

Of course, the real prize wasn't always the tuna or the Mahi—it was the shark. Mako and thresher sharks, to be specific. The meat of these guys is unreal. Think of swordfish steaks but with a bit more "wow" factor. You get that firm, steak-like texture and a flavor that leaves you wondering why anyone ever eats anything else. But most sharks are just disappointing. Their meat is soft, mushy, and tastes like something you wouldn't even feed to a raccoon. The ocean truly has a way of letting you know that not everything is worth catching. Still, pulling something huge from the deep was always a thrill, even if you had to suffer through a few shark duds along the way.

I don't mean to make it sound like I just tumbled out of the womb with a Penn International in one hand and a bucket of chum in the other. Like any skill worth a damn, fishing requires time and patience and more than a few painfully learned lessons along the way. There were days when I returned home empty-handed, the saltwater drenching my clothes and the sunburn reddening my skin, yet those experiences taught me more about persistence than any success ever could. Luckily for me, I had one hell of a teacher in my Uncle Pete.

That man had saltwater coursing through his veins and an almost preternatural grasp of all things ichthyological. Uncle Pete was a commercial fisherman, one of those gruff, no-nonsense types who'd spent more of his life on boats than dry land. He'd been working the waters off Rhode Island since before I was a twinkle in my daddy's eye, and there wasn't a creek or cove within 100 miles that he couldn't navigate with his eyes closed. To say he was an institution within the local fishing community would be an understatement. The man was a legend on the docks, spoken of with the kind of reverence usually reserved for saints and sea gods. With a rough exterior that belied a heart of gold, he took me under his wing from an early age, eager to pass on the secrets of the trade. Each trip out with him was a masterclass in patience, technique, and respect for the ocean's unpredictable nature. As we ventured farther from shore, he would regale me with stories of his younger years—tales of storms weathered, nets bursting with catches, and the camaraderie that existed among fishermen like a brotherhood bound by salt and sea. He taught me to read the water, to understand the whispers of the wind and the movements of fish below the surface. He would say, "You read the current, the breeze, the change in temperature, and the change in wind." Uncle Pete taught me to listen to the creaking of the boat, the engine, the moving parts. His lessons went far beyond fishing; they instilled in me a deep respect for nature, a sense of stewardship that persists to this day. The boat is always talking to you. Be ready to listen and answer her if needed.

The time spent on the water with Uncle Pete cemented in me a love for the sport that transcended mere pastime. It became a way of life, a connection to something larger than me. Each cast of the line became a prayer flung out into the universe, a hope that the mysteries of the deep might offer a glimpse of magic and mastery. As the sun dipped low, painting the sky in hues of orange and gold, I knew that I had found not just a hobby but a lifelong pursuit in the art of fishing—one that would keep calling me back to those open waters, time and time again.

I couldn't believe my luck when Uncle Pete took me under his barnacled wing. I knew I was learning from the best, and I soaked up his hard-won wisdom like a sponge. He taught me how to read the tides and the weather and how to spot the subtle signs of schooling bait fish and lurking predators. He showed me the proper way to rig a ballyhoo and the importance of keeping your hooks scary sharp.

But more than the technical stuff, what Uncle Pete really imparted was a bone-deep respect for the ocean and her creatures. Listening to his stories, I began to understand that fishing was about so much more than just hauling in the biggest trophy. It was about participating in an ancient dance, a timeless tango between human ingenuity and animal instinct. And like any good dance partner, you had to lead and follow in equal measure to know when to strike and when to shimmy.

I put those lessons to good use as I started to seriously pursue shark fishing in my early 20s. Now, most people hear "shark" and immediately picture that ominous fin slicing through the water, the duh-DUH duh-DUH theme from Jaws rising in the background. But the truth is, sharks are a lot more than just mindless killing machines. They're remarkable animals with complex behaviors and feeding patterns that you must understand if you hope to catch one.

The key to shark fishing, I quickly learned, is chumming. You must create a nice, pungent slick of mashed-up fish guts and blood to lure those toothy torpedoes to your bait. It's a messy, smelly business, but it's essential. Once you've got a good chum line going, you set up a float rig with a whole fish (usually a mackerel or false albacore) dangling at varying depths. Then, you sit back and wait for the magic to happen.

And when that magic does happen, hoo boy, you better be ready. A hooked shark will tail walk and greyhound across the surface like a demonically possessed Flipper. They'll burn, drag, and spool you to the backing in seconds flat if you don't have your thumbs clamped down hard on the reel. It's a herky-jerky, arm-wrenching battle if you're tangling with a big mako or thresher.

Ah, makos. Pound for pound, they just might be one of the most exhilarating fish I've ever tussled with. Built like missiles and meaner than hell, those crazy bastards never fail to put on an aerial show. They'll come rocketing out of the water in twisting somersaults, their jaws snapping like bear traps as they try to throw the hook. And if you're lucky enough to get one boat-side, you better watch your fingers and toes. Those gnashing teeth can make short work of an errant extremity.

But my God, are they delicious. Mako meat is like the filet mignon of the shark world—buttery, soft, and mildly sweet. After a successful hunt, there was nothing better than grilling up a few mako steaks right there at the dock, the lemon and butter sizzling, and the cold beers flowing. It always drew a crowd of wide-eyed onlookers, jaws hanging slack as they watched us carve up our quarry. "You guys actually EAT those things?" they'd ask, eyebrows arched in disbelief. "Hell yes, we do," we'd grin back, mouths full of tender, flaky flesh. As much as I love the adrenaline rush of shark wrangling, the ultimate angling high will always be chasing giant bluefin tuna. Those massive torpedoes of muscle are like the Moby Dicks of the modern sportfishing world - elusive, enigmatic, and capable of snapping you right back to reality quicker than you can say, "Call me Ishmael." Hooking into a giant bluefin is a bit like getting shot out of a cannon. One second, your rods are all bent over with the stately, rhythmic action of trolling. The next, you're hanging on for dear life as your reel screams like a bat out of hell. The first run alone can peel hundreds of yards of line in a finger-blistering blink. And that's just the beginning. Fighting a big tuna is an exercise in exquisite agony. You're locked in this intimate tango of give and take, your muscles straining against the raw power of an animal that can weigh as much as a grand piano. For hours, you'll crank and sweat and curse, your arms quivering like jelly as you try to make even an inch of headway. But slowly, one bicep-popping pump at a time, you'll start to gain ground.

I'll never forget the first bluefin over 250 pounds I managed to whip. It was a blustery fall day, the kind that lifeguards live for, with the wind howling and the whitecaps frothing. We were 92 miles off the Rhode Island coast, right on the edge of the continental shelf where the water drops off into the abyss. We'd been trolling all day with nothing but a few half-hearted nibbles to show for our efforts. But just as we were about to pack it in and head for home, one of our big squid spreader bar rigs just exploded.

After over an hour of fighting, the fish came greyhounding out of the chop like a Polaris missile, its sickle-shaped tail slicing through the spray. It must have made a dozen sizzling runs before we even got a glimpse of color. But finally, after what felt like a week of bicep-burning battles, we had it boatside—a fat, shimmering torpedo of a bluefin that taped out to 250 pristine pounds.

Hauling that bad boy through the tuna door was a religious experience. We whooped and hollered and pounded each other on the back like we'd just won the damn Super Bowl. And in a way, we had, but the fish wasn't done yet. It had one huge, last fight left in it, as it flopped and fought, streaking blood across the deck until it finally ran out of energy and was ours. A second round of celebration began. Besting a fish of that caliber is a once-in-a-lifetime achievement, the piscatorial pinnacle by which all other catches will forever be judged.

Of course, the real reward was yet to come. There's nothing on God's green earth quite like the taste of ultra-fresh bluefin sashimi, still twitching mere moments after it's been carved off the carcass. We feasted like ravenous Vikings right there on the dock, the translucent pink slices dissolving on our tongues like butter. It was the kind of decadent, primal thrill that you just can't replicate in any five-star joint. And after we'd had our fill, there were still over 100 tuna steaks to divvy up. Looking back, I realize how lucky I was to have those experiences and to commune with the ocean's apex predators in such an intimate way. It wasn't just about the adrenaline, bragging rights, or even the incomparable meals (though those were all nice perks). More than anything, fishing was my way of tapping into something elemental, something that reached beyond the topside tumult of human concerns.

When you're out there, locked in a muscle-searing death match with some hulking brute of the deep, all the petty anxieties and exhausting inanities of daily existence just sort of melt away. You're not a husband or a father or a provider; you're not a success or a failure or a cog in some corporate wheel. You're just a man with a line in the water, pitting your wits and your will against the implacable forces of nature. It's a humble reminder of our own puniness in the grand scheme of things.

And yet, in a funny way, it's also deeply empowering. Because when you do finally hoist that hard-won harvest over the door when you feel the solid thwack of a thick steak hitting the grill, you can't help but feel a surging sense of potency, of bone-deep competence. It's a feeling that bleeds over into every other aspect of your life, lending unshakable confidence to your step.

Perhaps that's the real gift of the angling life. Beyond all the fish tales, trophy shots, and manly misadventures, it teaches you to trust your gut and back your own horse, even when the odds are stacked against you. It shows you that you can reel in just about anything with enough tenacity, ingenuity, and sheer stubborn grit—be it a recalcitrant marlin or a record-breaking deal. So, to all my fellow anglers out there, whether you're chasing minnows or monsters, here's to the noble pursuit of fins and scales. May your lines always be tight and your drags always be screaming. And may the tales you tell forever grow longer in the retelling, as all good fish stories should.

As for me, you can bet your bottom dollar that I'll keep tilting at those watery windmills for as long as I can hold a rod. Because out there, dancing on the diamond-sparkling swells with my heart in my throat and my line stretched tight as piano wire, that's where I feel most alive, most fully myself.

And in the end, isn't that the best any of us can hope for? A place where we get to be exactly who we are, unburdened by expectations or explanations. For this brine-encrusted old salt, that place will always be smack dab in the middle of some sun-glazed, fish-rich sea.

A medium-size bluefin tuna, 256 pounds, still took an hour and a half to land, but the steaks and sushi were GREAT!

My 44-foot Post Sportfish "Relentless"—a great battlewagon

A mako jumping and trying to spit the hook.

CHAPTER 6:
MEETING CYNDI

Let me tell you something, amigo—there's no force on this green earth quite as potent or unpredictable as a pretty girl with a twinkle in her eye and a drink in her hand. You can be going about your business, minding your own rat race, when bam! Suddenly, there she is, all curves and coy smiles, and before you know it, you're throwing caution to the wind, and your best-laid plans out the porthole. That's just the nature of the beast we call chemistry, and oh boy, have I had my fair share of run-ins with those fickle temptresses.

But of all the chance encounters and near misses that have peppered my long and checkered romantic history, there's one that stands out like a beacon in the fog. One seemingly innocuous meeting would change the course of my life in ways I never imagined, even with a whole fistful of fairy dust and a direct line to Cupid himself. And it all started, as so many of my favorite stories do, with a bar and a babe.

Picture it: Narragansett, Rhode Island, sometime in the early 80s. I was slinging drinks at this beachside watering hole called The Point, a joint beloved by salty dogs and sandy butts. It was the kind of place where the jukebox played Springsteen, and the clientele thought Corona was an upscale brew. In other words, it was dive bar perfection.

Anyway, there I was, all of 21 and thinking I had the world by the short and curlies. I'd already been guarding for five seasons at that point and spent my winters cracking the books at URI, so I figured I pretty much had this whole life thing licked. It was a typical Wednesday night at The Point, all foam-flecked pitchers and slurred sea shanties. The Point was the kind of dive bar that had "legendary college hangout" written all over it. With the drinking age at 18, it was basically a free-for-all, and the place was always packed with a rotating cast of college kids who thought they were inventing fun every Wednesday night. Students were dancing like nobody was watching, playing pool like they were training for a pro league, and if the line outside got too long, there were always a few sneaky rebels finding their way through the unlocked back window—cue the bouncers, who, let's be honest, were probably getting as much exercise as we were. It was chaos, but the kind of chaos you'd trade your last textbook for.

Every bar around Narragansett had its own special night, and The Point was no slouch. We had the coveted 2-for-1 drinks because, apparently, nothing says "good decisions" like double-fisted cocktails. Schiller's was the home of "Beat the Clock" keg beer, where the price of a beer went up as the night went on. Twin Willows had half-price pitchers, which probably explains why so many people were doing keg stands by midnight. The Beachcomber, Bon View, and Caesar's all had their own specials, too, but honestly, I couldn't remember what they were half the time—too busy navigating specials and other distractions, like, you know, girls. Somehow, in the middle of all that, we were supposed to study? It's a miracle any of us graduated.

Then she walked in with her friend. Now, I know what you're thinking—like a typical guy, he thinks every remotely attractive female is some kind of Helen of Troy in hotpants. But trust me when I tell you, this girl was different. Oh, she was a looker all right, all sun-bleached hair and endless long legs, with four-inch heels that just wouldn't quit. But there was something else about her, a kind of inner glow that lit her up from the inside out like a Roman candle on the Fourth of July.

As she stepped through the door, the room seemed to hold its breath, the dim lighting catching the glimmer of her smile like it was the first light of dawn. I swear I could feel the atmosphere shift; a hush fell over the regulars, and it felt like the entire universe was unwinding in her presence for a moment. She wore a sundress that danced around her knees with every step, and the gentle sway of her hips was enough to send the jukebox into a frenzy all on its own.

I know it sounds clichéd, but I remember thinking that I had just witnessed the sun rise and set all at once. Her laughter rang out, vibrant and infectious, pulling me in like a siren's song. Patrons around the bar were drawn to her magnetic aura, but I got lost in that moment, the air charged with electricity. It was as if the world around us faded to black and white while she remained in vivid color.

With each passing second, I felt that familiar pull, the tugging at my heartstrings, urging me closer. I had to serve her, to be the one to hand her that first drink. Something about my intuition nagged at me, hinting that this wasn't just another ordinary night. This was different, and my life was about to take an unexpected detour.

Gathering my nerve, I smoothed my shirt, trying to play it cool despite the chaos spinning inside me. I approached her, my heart thudding like the beat of a rock band. "What can I get you?" I asked, trying to keep my voice steady, though I felt like a giddy schoolboy flirting with fate. She looked at me, those bright eyes sparkling like the ocean on a sunlit day, and my breath caught in my throat. "I'll have whatever you're having," she said with a mischievous grin, her voice warm and inviting, sending a shiver down my spine. There it was, that spark, that fleeting moment where everything just clicks. I poured her a drink, the glass clinks blending harmoniously with the laughter and raucous songs filling the bar. We began to chat while the other two bartenders took care of the customers, and before long, it felt like we were the only ones in the room. She shared stories about her summer adventures, tales that made me laugh so hard I nearly spilled my drink. (The owner was fine with his bartenders drinking if it encouraged the customers to drink more). In return, I mustered up tales of my own, weaving in just a touch of embellishment for dramatic effect—who doesn't love a good story?

Time seemed to stretch and bend around us, the world outside The Point feeling like it ceased to exist in the background. Just two slightly intoxicated souls bonding over shared laughter and undeniable chemistry. As the night wore on, the glow from those first encounters began to shimmer with potential, hinting at a future that felt as alluring as the moonlit waves crashing on the nearby shore.

Little did I know that one night—a simple, reckless indulgence—would become the cornerstone of the greatest chapter of my life. In that raucous bar, among the sea air and the lingering echoes of past heartbreaks, I felt as if I were on the cusp of a beautiful adventure that would redefine everything I thought I knew about love and fate. Her name was Cyndi. I would come to learn, and she was at the bar that night with a friend of hers. Some quiet lass who seemed to know every Tom, Dick, and Harry in the joint. But Cyndi, she held back a bit, perched on her stool like a white bird of paradise, just taking it all in with those cool, appraising eyes. Eyes that said, "I'm not impressed yet, but keep trying, you just might get there."

Well, let it be said that Ron Smith never backed down from a challenge. I sidled over to those two pretty birds and unleashed the full force of my considerable charm. I'm talking witty banter, rakish grins, the whole nine yards. And wonder of wonders, it seemed to be working! Cyndi started to unfurl a bit, leaning closer and batting those long enough lashes to rake clams. We talked and flirted and carried on until long after the last call had come and gone, the rest of the bar fading into irrelevance like so much sea foam on the breeze. By the time the grizzled old owner was giving us the stink eye and pointedly jangling his keys, I knew I had to see this girl again. There was just something about her, an indefinable spark that lit me up like a Roman Candle on the Fourth of July.

Lucky for me, Cyndi seemed to be picking up what I was putting down. We exchanged numbers on the back of a soggy cocktail napkin and made plans to meet up again soon. I floated home that night feeling ten feet tall and twice as charming, my head dizzy with the intoxicating brew of possibility and Pabst Blue Ribbon.

That was the start of a yearlong odyssey of beachy walks, midnight secrets, and long, languid afternoons spent tangled together while the rest of the world went about its workday business. Cyndi was unlike any girl I'd ever met before—funny and whip-smart but also almost preternaturally grounded. While I was busy spinning castles in the clouds and hatching harebrained schemes for the next big adventure, she gently tugged me back to earth, reminding me to enjoy the moment we were in.

Don't get me wrong, we had plenty of fun together. Many a weekend, we could be found cruising around in my old Camaro with the tunes cranked, chasing waves or cold brews depending on the day's forecast. I taught her how to waterski and showed off my cooking skills while she tried valiantly to civilize my caveman ways. We were young, salty, and sweet on each other, drunk on sun and skin, and the heady cocktail of raging hormones.

But even in the rosy, sand-strewn glow of those halcyon days, I could feel a restlessness starting to itch beneath my skin. A sense that as much fun as I was having playing house with this dream of a girl, there was a wide world out there just waiting to be explored and conquered. I was a boy-man still fumbling towards a sense of self, and as much as I cared for Cyndi represented a kind of stability I just wasn't ready to settle into, but I wasn't about to step out on her either. I'd been faithful to her for over a year, which is more than I can say for the other girls I dated back then. Cyndi was special, but I wasn't ready. At 23, I was pretty sure I had it all figured out— except for the part where I wasn't ready for a relationship. I was cocky, immature, and convinced that if I just put on enough cologne and flexed enough, I'd somehow be the next big thing. I had lofty goals—career goals, mostly. I was laser-focused on getting a job in real estate that made me feel important, even if it was just figuring out how to avoid answering emails for the first two years. Relationships? I wasn't even sure I could keep a houseplant alive. Honestly, I was more in love with the idea of a career than the idea of having someone who might expect me to, you know, listen and communicate. So, I dove headfirst into my super mature goal of "getting a career," meaning I spent more time at networking events than at my actual job. Turns out, maturity is a work in progress. Still, I was convinced I'd have it all figured out by 100, so no rush, right?

It didn't help matters that I had grown increasingly disillusioned with the whole college experience. While my buddies were busy funneling beers and chasing tail, I was fighting the urge to tear my hair out from sheer boredom and frustrated potential. It seemed like all my professors were either crusty old farts who hadn't seen the business end of the real world in decades or starry-eyed academics who wouldn't know a profit margin if it bit them in the elbow patches.

I'd sit in those stuffy lecture halls, half-listening to some droning dissertation on macroeconomic theory or some such nonsense, and feel the entrepreneurial juices withering on the vine. I knew in my gut that to really make my mark, I needed to be out there in the trenches, not stuck in some ivory tower circle jerk. The world was my oyster, and damned if I was going to let it turn to sand in my hands while I listened to those professors.

So, when an opportunity arose to cut bait on the whole college scene and strike out for the sunny shores of Florida and the Wild West of real estate, I lunged at it like a grouper at a shiny lure. My restless soul cried out for new horizons to conquer and mountains to climb. And if I'm being perfectly honest, a small, savage part of me was craving the completely untethered freedom of being a solo act once again.

I had a master plan: pack up my clothes, take $800 and my car, and drive straight to Florida like some kind of sun-seeking nomad with a spreadsheet. I'd spent months studying cities, towns, and developers as if I were about to become the world's youngest real estate mogul. I gave myself five years to earn $100,000 a year, which, let's be honest, was a lot of money back then—basically the 1986 equivalent of winning the lottery while driving a Ferrari. I figured I'd work my ass off, maybe wear a suit occasionally, and by the time I was 28, I'd be lounging on a yacht somewhere with a piña colada in hand. Well, spoiler alert: I hit $100,000 in year three, and it only went up from there. So much for the five-year deadline— I was like a time traveler who set an unrealistic goal and crushed it before the clock even ticked. Turns out, I've always had a knack for success. Sure, sometimes it took a little longer than expected—like that time I thought I could grow a full beard by my 25th birthday—but most of the time, I nailed my goals.

Breaking the news to Cyndi was one of the hardest things I've ever had to do. And believe me, I've done more than my fair share of difficult deeds. But looking into those fathomless eyes that had seen straight into my stormy core, I knew I had to come clean. She deserved the truth, even if it stung like a Portuguese man o' war.

I'll never forget that conversation, the two of us huddled together on "our" stretch of moonlit beach, the soft shushing of the waves, an incongruous soundtrack to the emotional tempest brewing between us. The moon hung low in the sky, casting a silvery glow that danced across the water, illuminating the doubts and fears flickering in my heart. I tried to explain as best I could, tripping over my tongue in my haste to make her understand. How do you articulate a storm? It wasn't her; it was me. I just needed to chart my own course for a while to test my mettle against the great wide open. I was like one of those damn seahorses, destined to drift untethered until I found my true purpose.

To her eternal credit, Cyndi took it like a champ. Oh, I could see the hurt swirling in those blue lagoons she called eyes, depths filled with unspoken dreams and shared laughter. But she bit her lip and nodded stoically as I babbled my semi-coherent explanations, each word feeling like a misstep on a tightrope strung high above the abyss of our relationship. I knew I was breaking her heart into a million little pieces, and the knowledge sat like a stone in my gut, heavy and unforgiving. It was a visceral ache, a reminder of all the moments we'd shared and all the promises now slipping through my fingers like grains of sand.

But I also knew, with the kind of unshakable conviction that only comes with the folly of youth, that to stay would have been a far greater betrayal, both to myself and to her. I could imagine a future—us, tied together like two vines entwined around the same tree—but the thought filled me with dread. For you see, as much as I cared for that golden girl with the world-wise eyes, I wasn't ready to be kept and grown and mature. Not yet, anyway. The wanderlust was strong in me, a wild beast clawing at the edges of my spirit, demanding to be free. I felt it calling, a siren song promising treasures unknown, adventures just beyond the horizon.

If I tried to ignore its call, I had no doubt that I'd end up resenting the hand that tried to hold me back, no matter how gentle its grasp. The visions of distant lands, unexplored trails, and sunrises in places I had yet to discover danced in my mind, mingling with a bit of guilt. It was almost cruel to have to choose between my desires and the happiness of someone I adored. No, best to make a clean break now, while we could both still walk away relatively unscathed. At that moment, under the watchful gaze of the stars, I resolved to honor both our truths: hers, filled with love and hope, and mine, yearning for something I couldn't yet define. As the final words slipped from my mouth, I braced myself for the inevitable silence that followed, a poignant lull that swallowed the sounds of the night. I watched as the light dimmed in her eyes, and the moon bore witness to our parting. The waves continued to crash, indifferent to our personal heartache, the tide pulling in and out, just as life would go on, relentless and unwavering. This was a moment etched in time, a bittersweet interlude in the symphony of our lives, and though it would leave scars, I hoped one day we would both look back on it as a necessary step on our journeys.

And so, I left, stuffing my raggedy duffel with a few t-shirts and some toiletries, cramming my oversized dreams into an undersized Camaro and pointing my prow towards the far-off port of possibility. I tried not to think about what (and who) I was leaving behind, focusing instead on the open road ahead and the fortune that lay waiting to be seized by my own two hands. But I'd be lying if I said Cyndi wasn't on my mind as those miles fell behind me. Her face would materialize unbidden in my rearview mirror, haloed by the setting sun and the whipping gold of cornfields, and my chest would tighten with an emotion I couldn't quite put a name to. Regret, longing, and nostalgia for something that hadn't even happened yet were a tangle of thorny sentiments that even my emotional machete couldn't quite hack through. What I didn't know then, what I couldn't possibly have foreseen as I chased the taillights of my own fate down I-95, was that our story was far from over. That wistful girl on the beach would reenter my life 13 years later, stepping back into the frame just when I needed her most. And this time, I'd be ready to be caught, hook, line, and sinker for the woman I'd let slip through my fingers so long ago.

But that, my friends, is a tale for another day and another chapter. First, I had some more living to do, and some hard-fought wisdom to earn in the trenches of young adulthood. The sea was calling, and it was high time this anchorless soul heeded its siren song at last. Little did I know how many leagues I'd have to sail before finding my way back to safe harbor.

Great times with Cyndi in Block Island

CHAPTER 7:
CARVING OUT A KINGDOM

The Eighties were incredible. Just saying it out loud conjures up visions of Gordon Gekko suspenders and "Greed is Good" grandstanding of cocaine-dusted Armani lapels and MTV moonmen. It was the decade of decadence, the era of excess, and damn if I didn't dive into that gilded pool headfirst without checking for rocks. The culture of the time crackled with energy, electric in its excess, resonating with the beat of synthesizers, power suits, and an unquenchable thirst for more money, more fame, more everything.

Fresh off my acrimonious academic abandonment and even fresher off my breakup with the college sweetheart I thought I'd left in the rearview, I hit the balmy shores of Boca like a man on a mission. And what a mission it was—to stake my claim on the New World of real estate riches and to piss on my territory like a young lion feeling the first stirrings of his own ferocity. I was fueled by a mix of youthful optimism and belly-sown determination; I was going to show them all, the naysayers and the haters, that I was a force to be reckoned with. I envisioned myself not just as a participant in the market but as a titan shaping the landscape of South Florida.

Those early days in Jupiter were a whirlwind of cramming and glad-handing, of burning the candle at both ends and then blowtorching the middle for good measure. I barely slept, hardly ate, just mainlined ambition with a Red Bull chaser and let the chips fall where they may. And fall they did, right into my eager little outstretched palms. Each phone call, each meeting, each frantic night spent poring over listings and prospects felt like a steppingstone on my path to greatness. The excitement was palpable, a rush akin to that of scoring a winning goal in the final seconds of a game.

You have to understand, South Florida in the mid-80s was like the Wild West for would-be cowboy capitalists like me. The streets were paved with foreclosures, with opportunity lurking around each corner, and the trees sprouted preconstruction contracts as if they were ripe for the picking. All you needed was a little chutzpah, a lot of elbow grease, and a steadfast refusal to take no for an answer. Luckily, I had all three in spades. Every day felt like a fierce competition, and I was training to be the last one standing. The locals whispered tales of deals gone wrong, and fortunes lost in the blink of an eye, yet I viewed those stories as nothing more than cautionary tales meant to fuel my hunger. Networking became my lifeline, and I immersed myself in the scene, attending every Schnitzel and Suds event or charity gala I could find. It was here, surrounded by ambitious entrepreneurs and seasoned investors, that I honed my pitch, learning the art of selling not just property but a vision of grandeur that everyone wanted to be a part of.

The thrill of the chase was intoxicating, often keeping me up at night as my mind raced through deals and possibilities. I remember the first time I closed on a property. The adrenaline was like a drug coursing through my veins. I could taste victory, sweet and intoxicating, as I signed those papers.

With each success, my confidence soared higher, and the dream of a luxurious lifestyle, where I could finally shed the lingering shadows of my past felt within reach. I was on the precipice of something monumental, and with every deal that fell into my lap, I felt myself edging closer to that elusive dream of wealth and status. The Eighties were just unfolding, and I was determined to write my own chapter in this storied decade of aspiration and ambition, defiant against anyone who dared to doubt me.

I started out as just another fresh-faced agent with more hair gel than experience, spending my days cold-calling expired listings and my nights networking with anyone who had a pulse and a checkbook. But I quickly realized that the real action was in development, in taking a piece of dirt and spinning it into gold brick by gilded brick. And that's where I found my true calling.

It was like a lightbulb went off over my head, illuminating the path to prosperity with its seductive, neon glow. Suddenly, I wasn't just some kid from Rhode Island with a copy of How to Win Friends and Influence People tucked under my arm. I was Ron Smith, real estate wunderkind, the guy who could smell a profitable deal from fifty paces and charm the pants off even the crustiest old planning board. The transformation was swift and intoxicating. I dove headfirst into the world of real estate, studying every angle, absorbing every scrap of knowledge I could find. I learned the lingo, mastered the market trends, and became a walking compendium of zoning laws and financing options. My phone buzzed constantly with leads, potential properties, and the latest gossip about who was selling and who was buying. I reveled in my newfound status, networking at the fanciest gala events, and rubbing shoulders with the rich and powerful, all while secretly dreaming of outdoing them.

I worked like a man possessed, which in hindsight, I probably was. Possessed by greed, by lust, by the sheer, unadulterated thrill of the chase. My mornings were consumed with meetings and coffee-fueled conversations with bankers and developers at trendy cafés. I'd sweet-talk them with charisma and confidence, my ambition radiating like an electric current. When the permits were slow to come through, I'd bulldoze my way to the front of the line, charming city officials with my boyish grin and a few well-placed compliments. Greasing palms and making promises became second nature; to me, every handshake was a new opportunity, every conversation a potential deal.

Then I'd spend my nights wining and dining investors at the hottest spots in town, where the champagne flowed as freely as the conversation. I'd regale them with grandiose tales of the fortune we'd make together, spinning narratives that danced on the edge of reality. "Just sign on the dotted line, my friend, and we'll be off to the races!" I urged them, drawing them into my vision of success.

And sign they did. Faster than you could say, "adjustable rate mortgage," I had a booming business and a burgeoning reputation. The deals got bigger, the stakes higher, and I rode that rocket ship of success straight to the penthouse suite. I remember the day I bought my first Rolex before I turned 25, a gleaming testament to my Midas touch and unquenchable thirst for status symbols. Every tick of that watch was a reminder of my accomplishments, my social ascent. With each month, my bank account grew, as did my expectations and desires.

I also had my first home, a waterfront home on a canal. But it wasn't enough; it was never enough. Each conquest only fed the beast, stoking the flames of my ambition until it roared with an insatiable hunger. I needed more deals, more profits, more wins, goddammit! I became like a great white shark, forever prowling the shallows for my next meal, perpetually restless, never slowing down. Nights spent in my office strategizing were just as thrilling as the late-night parties that followed. I lived for the adrenaline, the rush of closing a deal, of outmaneuvering the competition. And oh, what meals they were! South Florida in the mid-80s was a nonstop bacchanal of excess and extravagance, a never-ending parade of fast cars and faster women. The city pulsed with energy; its vibrant nightlife was an intoxicating cocktail of glitz and glamor.

There were nameless, faceless flings and short-lived romances, partners in crime who drifted in and out of my life as quickly as the money flowed in. I reveled in the attention, a self-proclaimed king of the night, yet nothing ever stuck—the heart I built around myself remained fortified against any real connection. I shielded my vulnerabilities with bravado, convinced that ambition was the only kind of love I'd ever need. Each time someone tried to break through my fortress, I pushed them away with a smile, insisting I was fine. After all, who needs a real relationship when you have the intoxicating allure of ambition and excess at your fingertips? As the sun set, casting a golden hue over my world of luxury, I couldn't help but chase after the next high, believing it was only a matter of time before I found what I was truly missing. Yet deep down, a flicker of doubt began to stir—was this all there was?

The truth was, I was married to the game, wed to the pursuit of that next big score. Everything else was just white noise, the collateral damage of a life lived in overdrive. I didn't have time for pesky things like balance or self-reflection. I was going to be somebody, and I didn't care how many somebodies I had to steamroll to get there.

And it was working, too. By the time I hit 30, I'd traded in my starter Rolex for a presidential model, upgraded the Thunderbird to a Cadillac, and moved my home base back up to Rhode Island, the prodigal son returning to lord over his dominion.

But even as I sat in my office, feet propped up on a desk that cost more than some people's cars, I couldn't shake the feeling that something was missing. It was like this hollow space behind my breastbone, a yawning chasm that no deal-chasing or trophy-acquiring could quite fill. I'd spent so long sprinting toward the horizon that I'd never stopped to savor the scenery along the way.

And what scenery it was! The people I'd known, the experiences I could have had if I hadn't been so hell-bent on world domination. The quieter joys of companionship and connection, of lazy Sundays and long talks over even longer wine. All the things that make life rich and textured and meaningful, are sacrificed on the altar of ambition without a second thought.

I think a part of me knew, even then at 35, that I was hurtling towards some kind of reckoning. That the fire I was fueling with hopes and Grey Goose was bound to consume me if I didn't find a way to bank it soon. But I was like Icarus in Ferragamos, flying too close to the sun and too in love with the heat to pull away.

And so, I kept on, riding the wave of my hubris higher and higher. But I still wasn't happy. For now, I'll simply say this to any young buck out there with dollar signs in his eyes and the world at his feet: Chase the dream. Build that empire brick by back-breaking brick. But don't forget to build a life along the way. Because at the end of the day, when you're sifting through the rubble of your own ambitions, it's not the size of your kingdom that will define you.

It's the quality of your reign.

Always shoot for the top. It's the only way of true success.

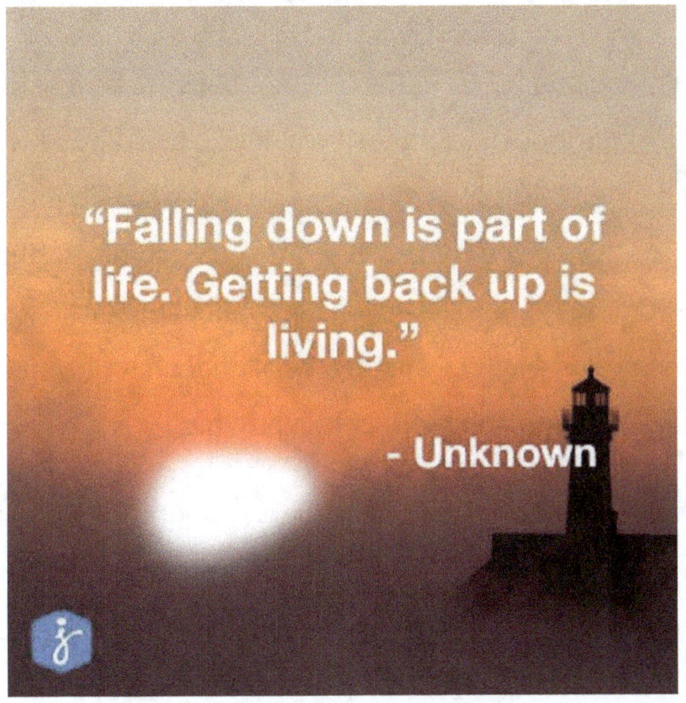

Life is great if you work hard and never let it get you down.

CHAPTER 8:
FIRST MATE FOR LIFE

They say the sea is a harsh mistress, demanding and unforgiving in her affections. But I've always found her to be a most generous lover, bestowing her bountiful gifts on those bold enough to brave her tempestuous embrace. And of all the treasures she's seen fit to grant me over the years, none shines brighter or feels more precious than the one I found in a most unexpected place—a sticky Formica booth in a Rhode Island Dunkin' Donuts.

It was the summer of '98 and I was back in my old stomping grounds, taking a break from the breakneck pace of my Florida real estate juggernaut. Thirteen years had passed since I'd left a certain long-haired girl crying on the beach as I chased my fortune down the coast. I'd be lying if I said I hadn't thought about Cyndi in the intervening years, hadn't wondered what might have been if I'd been a little less stubborn and hell-bent on proving myself to the world.

But those were idle daydreams, the wistful musings of a man too busy building an empire to dwell on the detritus of his romantic past. Or so I thought until fate saw fit to plant a woman's size nine boat shoe squarely in my unsuspecting ass.

I was standing in line, impatient to order a Boston cream, minding my own post-deal fatigue. A woman in line in front of me was tan with legs for days and a figure that could stop traffic. Her hair was cut short in a pixie cut, which is not my favorite style for a woman, but then she turned around, and everything filtered through the hiss of an espresso machine and the clamor of a busy donut shop. A voice that had once whispered sweet nothings in my eager ear and then fought back tears as I packed my worldly belongings into a beat-up Chevy said, "Ron? Ron Smith? Is that you?"

There, standing in line not ten feet away, a vision in beautiful, fitted jeans, four-inch pumps, and a disbelieving grin was Cyndi. My Cyndi. Only, not a girl anymore but a woman, all grown up and glowing with an inner light that was altogether entrancing. Time seemed to slow as we stared at each other, the years melting away like so much sugar in a steaming cup of joe. At that moment, it was as if no time had passed at all, as if we were still those two sunburned kids necking under the boardwalk and dreaming of a future that seemed as vast and dazzling as the Atlantic stretching out before us. I don't remember who moved first, but suddenly, we were hugging, laughing, tripping over our words in our eagerness to catch up. She was in the middle of a divorce, she told me, her voice catching only slightly on the word. I was unattached, having recently extricated myself from yet another go-nowhere relationship with a woman who couldn't see past my wallet. The stars, it seemed, had finally aligned.

We sat in that Dunkin' Donuts for hours, oblivious to the annoyed glances of the afternoon coffee crowd. We talked about everything and nothing, falling effortlessly into the old rhythms of gentle teasing and soul-baring confession. It was as if no time had passed, yet we were clearly different people than the lovesick kids who had parted ways on that moonlit beach so long ago.

I looked at Cyndi, really looked at her, and marveled at the myriad ways she had changed. She was still breathtaking, with that honeyed hair and mermaid eyes that could drown a man at twenty paces. But there was a quiet assurance to her now, a hard-won wisdom that sat lightly on her sun-freckled shoulders. This was a woman who had been through some shit, who had looked life square in the eye and refused to blink first. And I suddenly found that combination of strength and softness unutterably sexy.

In the days that followed, we were inseparable. We met to have coffee and talk. I told her about my business triumphs and my existential angst, and spilled my guts about the gnawing emptiness that all the deal-chasing and glad-handing could never quite fill. She listened with that patented Cyndi combination of empathy and no-bullshit pragmatism, offering insights that cut straight to the marrow of my dilemmas. Then she told me she had a special needs son who was only three years old at this time, and she was in the process of a divorce. I sensed she needed some space to heal, but we would still meet, keeping our relationship as nothing more than close friends until she got everything settled. For her part, she confided in me about her own journey—the challenges of single motherhood, the loneliness of a marriage gone sour, and the quiet determination that had propelled her to carve out a successful career in her own right. I was blown away by her resilience and uncanny ability to wrest triumph from the clenched jaws of adversity. This was a woman to be reckoned with and I found myself falling for her all over again, only harder this time because I finally understood how rare and precious a gift she truly was.

As the weeks turned into months, it became increasingly clear that this wasn't just some flukish rekindling of an old flame. This was the real deal, the once-in-a-lifetime connection that poets write sonnets about, and fools spend their whole lives chasing. Cyndi got me in a way that no one else ever had, saw through the bluster and the bullshit to the scared little boy hiding behind the bravado. She let me be myself, never attempting to change me. She shoved me off the proverbial cliff when I needed it–encouraging me to go into millions of dollars in debt to make an investment–and she'd keep me from diving off the deep end when she felt I was making a hasty decision. Cyndi's always right, and I trust her. And miracle of miracles, she loves me exactly the way I am. I knew I couldn't let her slip through my fingers again. Knew it with the same bone-deep certainty that had propelled me through a hundred boardrooms and over a thousand hurdles. This woman was my destiny, and I'd be damned if I was going to miss my shot at happiness because I was too proud or too stubborn to grab it with both hands.

So, I did the only thing a smitten man could do: ask her to marry me. But not before I'd sought out the blessing of the one man whose opinion mattered more than any other: Cyndi's father, Leo.

Now, I've stared down some hard cases in my day, and negotiated with sharks in Saville Row suits who would just as soon stab you in the back as shake your hand. But none of them compared to the sheer pants-pissing terror I felt as I sat across from Leo, my palms sweating and my collar suddenly too tight. This was the man who had raised the love of my life and instilled in her the values of hard work and integrity that I so admired. His good opinion meant the world to me, and I was determined to win it fair and square.

"Leo," I began, my voice only quavering slightly. "I love your daughter more than life itself. She's my true north, my safe harbor in the storm. I know I wasn't good enough for her all those years ago, but I'm a different man now. A better man, because of her… And if you give me your blessing, I promise to spend the rest of my days making sure she knows just how cherished she is."

Leo eyed me for a long moment, his expression inscrutable behind his wire-rimmed glasses. I could feel my heart hammering against my ribcage, my mouth dry as the Sahara at high noon. And then, just when I thought I might pass out from the sheer suspense of it all, he cracked a smile that was equal parts wry and welcoming.

"Took you long enough," he said, his eyes twinkling with a mischief that was so like his daughter's. "I always knew you two would find your way back to each other. You have my blessing, son. Just don't screw it up this time."

I nearly wept with relief, my laughter watery as I pumped his hand with a fervor that was only slightly awkward. I had gotten my girl and my dream, and I knew enough to hang onto both for dear life.

Our wedding was a small, intimate affair, just close friends and family. We didn't need the pomp and circumstance, the cast of thousands, and the overblown fripperies. All we needed was each other, the salt-tang air, and the certain knowledge that we were precisely where we were meant to be.

The only way to get invited to our wedding was to know Gregory. I fell in love with him as much as I fell in love with Cyndi (he lived with us until he was 22), and we both agreed that every single guest needed to be someone who truly knew him—no distant relatives or acquaintances we only saw at weddings or funerals. This was going to be an intimate affair, and we were determined to keep it that way. We made the decision early on to pay for everything ourselves, despite our parents repeatedly offering to help. We knew that if anyone else contributed, we'd be obligated to invite people like Aunt Gertrude and Uncle Simon, and that wasn't part of our vision. When our parents came to us, with their soft voices and tentative questions about whether certain people were on the guest list, it became a bit of a game to say, "No." Soon, they became the front line of defense, standing firm like football players, explaining that we were keeping the guest list small. In the end, the total headcount was 101, and we had an amazing time—just the people who mattered most to us, celebrating in exactly the way we wanted.

When Cyndi appeared on her father's arm, resplendent in a simple sheath that hugged her curves like the morning mist, I thought my heart might burst from sheer, unmitigated joy as I stood there in my kilt. This was really happening. This gorgeous, whip-smart, endlessly fascinating creature had agreed to be my partner, my copilot on the great adventure of life. I was the luckiest son of a bitch on the planet, and I knew it.

We exchanged vows with the sniffles of our assembled loved ones punctuating our heartfelt words. And then, just as the sun began its descent into the blushing sea, something magical happened. From somewhere behind us, the strains of a bagpipe began to curl through the salt-soaked air, the haunting melody sending chills racing up my spine.

I turned to Cyndi, my eyes wide with wonder and my heart nearly bursting with gratitude. Even after all this time, she remembered how much my Irish heritage meant to me. Had gone out of her way to arrange this special surprise, this pitch-perfect grace note that elevated an already perfect day into the realm of the unforgettable.

As the piper played us down the aisle, his kilt snapping in the breeze and his cheeks ruddy with exertion, I squeezed my new wife's hand and mouthed a silent, "Thank you." She simply smiled, that knowing, enigmatic Mona Lisa smile that said, "I get you," "You're welcome," and "I love you, you big galoot," all at once.

And I knew, with a certainty that reverberated in my bones, that I had finally found my home, my anchor, my true port in the storm. We went straight to the reception afterward, surprising our guests. Cyndi and I didn't want to miss the party while we were off taking wedding photos for hours, keeping everyone waiting for us. And the whole point of paying for the damn thing ourselves was to do it our way, so we started a new tradition—we corralled the best man and the best woman, hopped in a limo about three hours before the ceremony started, went to the large grounds overlooking Narragansett Bay in Newport, and took all the photos before we were legally wed. Trust me, my smile couldn't have been any wider either way. I'd found the anchor to my ship, and she was proud to attach herself to me to become a team.

That entire day is one of the happiest on record. There may have been a bit of wine and champagne at the photoshoot, so of course, by the time the limo pulled into the St. Thomas More Church, nature called. I ran off to find the facilities to relieve myself, and more than a few people caught a glimpse of Cyndi standing with her father, and I was nowhere to be found. Whispers fluttered that I may have stood her up—as if such a thing might ever happen. I burst through a side door, and the wedding ceremony flew by. As we began our march down the aisle as Mister and Missus, bagpipes began playing. I assumed they were coming through the speakers, but when we exited the church, there was a proper Scotsman in a kilt, sweater, hat, socks, purse, and suspenders playing an upbeat ditty on the bagpipes. In the years since that magical day of reconnection in the Dunkin' Donuts, my love and appreciation for Cyndi has only grown deeper, richer, and more textured with each passing season. She is my best friend, staunchest ally, fiercest defender, and most enthusiastic cheerleader. She is the calm to my storm, the good sense to my harebrained scheming. She is, in short, the best damn first mate a salty old sea dog like me could ever hope for.

It doesn't hurt that she's taken to the boating life like a duck to water, either. From the moment she first stepped foot on my beloved vessel, Cyndi has been a quick study with an innate feel for the rhythms and demands of life on the high seas. She can read a tide chart like a Homeric epic and can spot a gathering squall from a nautical mile away. She has an uncanny knack for anticipating what needs to happen three steps before it does, a preternatural grasp of the physics and poetry of a well-run ship. Cyndi can read and interpret any instrument on the boat to get us to our destination, and she's also great at using a chart for currents, wind, and foggy destinations.

But more than just her technical proficiency makes Cyndi such an invaluable partner on the water. It's her unflappable nature, her ability to keep a cool head when others (me included) might be on the verge of losing theirs entirely. I can't tell you how many times she's talked me down from the ledge when a mechanical failure or a navigational snafu had me ready to abandon ship and swim for shore. She is the steady hand on the tiller, the voice of reason cutting through the wind and the bluster.

And when the chips are down, and the waves are high, there's no one I'd rather have by my side than Cyndi. We've weathered our share of storms together, both literal and figurative, and each time, we come through stronger, surer of our ability to handle whatever the sea or life might throw our way. We move in perfect synchronicity, anticipating each other's needs and responding with a wordless ease that can only be born of true intimacy and trust.

I'll never forget the time we were making a tricky crossing from Newport to Block Island, the chop so rough and the visibility so poor that even I was starting to doubt the wisdom of pressing on. But Cyndi never wavered, never gave so much as an inch to the rising panic that threatened to engulf us both. She just hunkered down at the helm with me, her jaw set and her eyes fixed on the horizon, calling out course corrections and words of encouragement in equal measure. She would read out the course and look for lobster pots, and I would handle the waves, rain, fog, current, or wind.

And when we finally made landfall, battered but unbroken, she turned to me with that same steady gaze and said, "We make a hell of a team, you and me. There's nothing we can't handle as long as we do it together." I could only nod, too choked up to speak, too full of awe and gratitude for this remarkable woman who had chosen, against all odds and good sense, to cast her lot with mine.

But it's not just Cyndi's toughness and tenacity that makes her such a remarkable partner, both on the water and off. It's her compassion, her empathy, her ability to see beneath the surface of things to the beating heart that lies beneath. I may be the one who can read a marina like a book, who can size up a mark and close a deal before the ink is dry on the contract. But Cyndi is the one who can read people, who can sense the hidden hurts and secret dreams that drive us all.

I am a truer and more fully realized version of myself. She challenges me to be kinder, gentler, more patient, and understanding. She calls me on my bullshit and celebrates my victories with equal fervor. She is my shining example of what it means to live with integrity, with purpose and passion, and an unyielding commitment to leaving the world a little better than you found it. She has never tried to change me, allowing me to express my boisterous laughter and flirtatious nature.

"You can always look at the menu; you just can't order anything," she likes to say.

As I look back on the winding road that led me to this point, to this life, and this love that I could never have foreseen all those years ago, I am struck by the sheer improbability of it all. The odds that two starry-eyed kids from opposite sides of the tracks would find each other, lose each other, and then find each other again in the fullness of time and experience. The serendipity of that chance encounter in a donut shop, the courage it took for both of us to open our hearts once more to the possibility of forever. It has been 25 years since our vows were spoken, and God willing, we'll last another 25. She is my anchor, and this old sea dog needs something to hold him down. Cyndi is the sweet siren song that always beckons me home. She is the land to my sea, the keeper of my heart.

But perhaps that's the greatest lesson that Cyndi and the sea have taught me over the course of our many voyages together. That joy, like treasure, is often found in the most unexpected of places. That the truest and most lasting forms of wealth are not measured in dollars or deals but in moments of connection, of grace, of sheer, unmitigated gratitude for the gift of another day spent in pursuit of one's passions with the love of one's life by their side.

And so, my friends, as I look out over the bow of my ship and contemplate the endless blue horizon that stretches before us, I am filled with a sense of peace and purpose that I never knew I was seeking. For I know that whatever storms may come, whatever waves may rise to meet us, I have my first mate and my guiding star right beside me, her hand firmly clasped in mine, her eyes fixed on the same far distant shore.

Cyndi, my love, my partner, my friend. Thank you for being my safe harbor and my home. Thank you for setting out on this grand adventure with me, weathering the squalls, savoring the sunsets, and never losing sight of the true treasure in the journey itself. Thank you for loving me, not despite my flaws and foibles and irritability that make me who I am, but because of them, for seeing the man I was always meant to be and helping me to become him.

And most of all, thank you for being you. For being the rarest and most precious of gems, a woman of strength, substance, and an unwavering moral compass. For being the kind of person who makes everyone around her want to be better, do better, live and love with more abandon and less fear.

As we set sail on this next chapter of our voyage together, I am filled with a sense of excitement and possibility that I haven't felt since I was a young man with the world at his feet. Only now, I know that I don't have to conquer that world alone. I have my soulmate by my side, my port in every storm, my love and my light.

So fair winds, my darling, let's see where this wild, wondrous journey takes us next. I promise to be the captain and companion you and I deserve to the very last drop of water over the hull. No looking back now. The horizon, blue and unbounded, beckoned us forward into the untold stories yet to be written.

A bagpiper who looked similar to the one I was surprised with at the wedding

On a catamaran exploring around Santorini, Greece

The three musketeers. Gregory, my stepson is about 10 years old.

CHAPTER 9:
DARK DAYS AND NEW BEGINNINGS

Life has a way of throwing curveballs when you least expect them and pulling the rug out from under you just when you think you've figured it all out. I've had my share of hard knocks over the years—everyone does, I suppose. They made me stronger, and they also made me want to experience everything in life, So I steadily checked things off my bucket list, which was mostly related to the ocean and solitude on the sea. But there was a stretch in the early-to-mid 2000s that felt like a perfect storm of pain and upheaval, like the universe was conspiring to break me down so I could build myself back up again.

It started with my sister Linda. She was 35 years old, the picture of health and vitality. A loving wife, a doting mother to three beautiful children, the kind of person who lit up a room just by walking into it. And then, out of nowhere, the hammer blow fell— advanced colon cancer, stage four. I remember getting the call from her husband, hearing the words but not quite processing them. Cancer. Linda. It didn't compute. How could someone so young, so full of life, be struck down by something so cruel and indiscriminate? It felt like a sick cosmic joke, a glitch in the matrix of the universe.

But it was all too real. The next two years were a blur of hospital visits and somber conversations, of watching helplessly as my little sister wasted away before my eyes. She fought like a warrior, enduring round after round of chemo and radiation, surgery after surgery. But in the end, even her indomitable spirit wasn't enough to keep the disease at bay.

She passed away on a sunny day in April 2001 while I was visiting her in hospice care. Her body, ravaged by cancer, had little left to give, but she was an organ donor, nonetheless. The interns rushed into the room to collect her still-warm body and found something precious worth saving—her eyes. They moved with quiet efficiency, transferring my sister's eyes into a small cooler. Within moments, they were gone, leaving only the faintest trace of her presence behind. A sense of finality hung in the air, but little did we know that her gift was just beginning to unfold.

Within the next year, two letters arrived at John's house, each one from a stranger whose life had been touched by Linda's final act of kindness. The first came from a 43-year-old man who had lost his sight two decades earlier. With one of Linda's eyes, he could see again. His words were simple but filled with deep gratitude. A few months later, a second letter arrived, this time from a 57-year-old man who had lived in darkness for years. Both letters were heartwarming reminders that Linda's spirit still had the power to bring light to others. As we read their words, it felt like Linda was seeing the world again through the eyes of those she had helped.

She was only 37 years old when she passed. Her twins had just turned seven, and her little girl was only five. I remember holding them as they cried, these small, bewildered creatures who couldn't quite grasp the magnitude of what they'd lost. And I remember thinking, through my own haze of grief, that I had to be strong for them, had to step up and be the rock that Linda had always been for me.

But the truth was, I was barely keeping it together myself. Losing Linda shattered me in ways I couldn't fully articulate, even to myself. She had been my first anchor, my true north, the one person who could always talk me down from the ledge when my impulsiveness and self-destructive tendencies threatened to get the best of me. Cyndi is great at keeping me cool, but not like Linda. My sister could recognize the roiling anger bubbling under the surface and steer me back to calm waters before I blew a gasket. I thought back to all the times she'd bailed me out of trouble, all the times she'd let me crash on her couch when I was too drunk or high to make it home. She never judged, never lectured, just handed me a cup of coffee and a word of gentle advice. "You've got to take better care of yourself, big brother," she'd say, her eyes full of love and worry. "You're no good to anyone if you're running on empty."

I'd always brushed off her concerns with a laugh and a shrug, convinced of my own invincibility. But now, standing at her graveside and watching her casket being lowered into the ground, the crushing weight of my own mortality hit me like a freight train. I was 40 years old, and I'd been burning the candle at both ends for as long as I could remember. How much longer could I keep going before I ended up like Linda, cut down in the prime of life by my own neglect and abuse?

The thought terrified me but also sparked something deep inside—a flicker of determination, a burning need to make a change before it was too late. I couldn't keep living the way I had been, chasing deals and downing drinks like there was no tomorrow. I had to find a way to slow down, to focus on what really mattered, before I self-destructed completely.

But old habits die hard, and the lure of numbness was strong. I told myself I could handle it, that I was in control, even as the evidence mounted to the contrary. And then, a hammer blow fell. I was 54 years old, and my liver failed. The years of hard living had finally caught up with me, and my body was shutting down. I remember lying in that hospital bed, jaundiced and weak, listening to the doctor's grim prognosis. If I didn't stop drinking, I'd be dead within a year. If I did stop, there would be a good chance that I could live a long, healthy life.

I had never felt any signs of liver failure coming. In fact, I had been living it up until the day after the St. Patrick's Day festivities and parade in Newport, where the bars open at 9 a.m., and the parade kicks off at 11 a.m., no matter what the weather decides to throw at us. And trust me, Newport has seen it all. I've been to parades in blizzards, and torrential rain, and once, I swear it was 10 degrees above zero with a wind chill that could freeze your thoughts mid-sentence. But it doesn't matter—when you're in Newport on St. Patrick's Day, everyone is Irish. That year, Cyndi and I were with Gary, Steve, and their wives, Sharon and Wanda, trying to dodge the crowds spilling out of bars as they stumbled to their prime viewing spots for the parade. And let's not forget the food— corned beef and cabbage served with a side of questionable decisions. As we all gathered for the festivities, Cyndi proudly claimed her title as the Designated Driver, which in Newport is just code for "a person who isn't drunk enough to think it's a good idea to walk through the parade route." But hey, someone's got to be the responsible one while the rest of us pretend that our Irish roots are directly linked to our ability to consume an absurd amount of Guinness and whiskey before noon.

I was feeling great. We all somehow managed to stay upright and make it through a full day of festivities, which was a small miracle considering how much we were trying to drink like we were still in college. By the end of the day, I didn't even remember what I was supposed to be feeling or thinking, just that I had somehow survived the kind of day that makes you question if your liver is even real.

Well, the next day I woke up feeling like I'd just been hit by a freight train—chills, sweats, shakes, the whole works. Then the real fun began: vomiting and… well, let's just say the other end wasn't exactly cooperative either. After a few hours of feeling like a human rollercoaster, Cyndi decided I should probably see a doctor, so I went off to the emergency room. They hooked me up to fluids like I was some sort of human water balloon, and then, as luck would have it, a gastroenterologist walked in. This guy looked at all the tests, scratched his head, and told me I had liver failure from cirrhosis. "Great," I thought. "What's next, doc? Am I getting a liver transplant or a punch card for frequent hospital visits?"

Ten days later, I was out of the hospital, and the doc sent me off to an outpatient addiction facility for a little "just in case" assessment. I sat down with a guy who could've been a therapist, a life coach, and possibly the world's best bartender, all rolled into one. After three hours of chatting, he told me, "You're not an alcoholic; you just love to drink and party. Now stop drinking, and go live your life." And that's it. I quit drinking immediately because I have always had a strong mind and unmatched willpower. I dabbled in mind-altering substances until I entered the corporate world—quit cold turkey. Smoked a cigarette or ten while bartending, but when I heard Linda's diagnosis, I never so much as craved a cigarette ever again. That's how I work. If the drink was trying to kill me, our drinking days were over. Simple as that. I built my weak body back into shape, and most people don't know only 20% of my liver is working. The rest is full of cirrhosis, and I take a dozen pills a day.

It's been nine years since I had my last drink. Never craved it, never wanted it. In fact, I'm now always the designated driver. My friends love me for it. I go to bars, parties, St. Patrick's Day parades, and I'm as sober as a judge. You'd think I'd be tempted, right?

Nope. I'm out there dancing like I'm auditioning for Dancing with the Stars, shaking it like nobody's business. I might be the only sober person at a bar who looks like they're on a three-day bender. I'm living my life to the fullest. I'll tell you this: my "spigot" is in full operation.

That's right—one twist, and the desire to drink is gone forever. As for my friends? Well, they're still out there trying to have their fun. I'm just the guy with a ginger ale in one hand and a dance move that says, "I'm having more fun than you."

But even after I swore off alcohol forever, other challenges began to pile up. My stepson Gregory, who was born with cerebral palsy, was requiring more care and attention as he grew older. His needs were complex and ever-changing, and navigating the maze of doctors, therapists, and special education programs was a full-time job.

Cyndi, once again, stepped up in a big way. She'd always been an incredible mother, never losing her ambition and vitality. Watching Cyndi's devotion to her son lit a fire under me to be a better husband and stepfather at 40. I'd always loved Gregory fiercely, but I'd been more of a fun dad than a hands-on one, leaving the day-to-day heavy lifting to Cyndi. I started attending Gregory's doctor's appointments and more of his therapy sessions, learning everything I could about his condition and what we could do to support his development. I took over more of the household chores and errands, freeing up Cyndi to focus on Gregory's care. And then, in 2002, just a year after Linda passed away, I had a chance to put that realization into practice in a big way. It was the peak of summer, and I'd planned a boating trip to Block Island and Martha's Vineyard for a 10-day period to take a break from the heaviness of grief, with some friends, their children, Gregory, and Linda's twins. (After all, I am the GREAT UNCLE RON.)

We set out with a group of five boats, all of us with children around the same age, looking forward to a week of sun and sand and laughter. But 4 days into our arrival at Champlin's Marina, we found chaos and confusion. A fire had broken out in the laundry house, and the whole place was swarming with firefighters and Coast Guard personnel.

At first, we thought we'd just wait it out, let the authorities do their thing, and then set up camp on the beach on that beautiful 5th of July. But as the hours ticked by and the smoke continued to billow, it became clear that this was no ordinary blaze. The laundry house was a total loss, and the marina was shut down indefinitely.

For a moment, I felt the old frustration and impatience rising, the urge to just push through and make it work somehow. But then I took in those kids and their wide eyes and frustrated looks over an end to their fun. I knew that the last thing they needed was more uncertainty and upheaval. We stayed and watched as the firefighters drained the pool to fight the blaze. The excitement of it meant that the kids were no longer heartbroken--the fire didn't matter to them, but the draining of the pool did.

We chatted about it as we pivoted, loading everyone back onto the boats and setting a course for Martha's Vineyard instead. It was a longer trip than expected. About halfway on the 20-mile journey, a large, dark storm blew through, though it hadn't been on any weather report. Waves built to eight-foot rollers, and the rain came in sideways. Fortunately, the squall left as fast as it came, lasting 15 minutes at most. Although we arrived well past dark, the kids were troopers. They helped us navigate by flashlight, giggling and chattering with excitement. And over the next few days, as we explored the island together, I watched something amazing happen. Those kids, who had been through so much heartache and loss, began to come alive again. They laughed, played, and chased each other through the dunes, and their faces lit up with a joy that had been missing for far too long.

It hit me, then, how much power we each have to shape the world around us and create moments of beauty and connection even in the darkest times. I'd spent so many years focused on what I could get, on what I could achieve and acquire. But in that moment, watching those kids splash in the surf and build sandcastles in the sun, I realized that the most important thing I could do was give—my time, my attention, my love.

It was a revelation that stayed with me long after we returned home, a north star that guided me through the twists and turns of my own healing journey. I knew, now, that I didn't want to go back to the way things had been before— the long hours, the constant hustle, the numbing and escapism. I wanted to build a life rich in meaning and purpose, allowing me to use my gifts in service of something greater than myself.

And slowly but surely, that's what I began to do. I focused on rebuilding my health and relationships, being present and engaged with the people who mattered most to me. I continued my volunteer work with certain environmental groups, and I found myself drawn more and more to the idea of making boating and the ocean a central part of my life again. I thought back to that trip to Martha's Vineyard, to the joy and resilience I'd seen in those kids. And I knew that I couldn't let them down, that I had to keep fighting for the life I wanted, the life Linda would have wanted for me and her children. And so, bit by bit, day by day, I began to craft a new identity for myself, one that blended my love of the water with my desire to make a difference in the world. I still had my own successful real estate business, but I couldn't stop thinking about Florida and boat deliveries. As my move to Florida got closer, I thought about how I could combine both endeavors to allow me to share my passion with others while also making a living. Those early days were a blur of hard work, steep learning curves, long hours, and lean times. But through it all, I felt a sense of rightness, a deep knowing that I was exactly where I was meant to be. And as my business began to grow and thrive, as I watched my clients' faces light up with joy and wonder at the beauty of the water, I knew that all the struggles and sacrifices had been worth it.

Looking back now, I can see how those dark days of loss and reckoning were the crucible that forged me into the man I am today. They stripped me down to my essence, and forced me to confront the parts of myself I'd been running from for so long. In the process, they opened me up to new possibilities and new ways of being in the world.

I've learned to lean into discomfort, to face my fears head-on, and keep moving forward. And I've learned, too, that the greatest joys and triumphs often come on the other side of the deepest pain and struggle.

So, to anyone out there who's facing their own dark days, their own moments of upheaval and uncertainty, I say this: keep going. Keep putting one foot in front of the other, and keep reaching out for help and support when you need it. And trust that, even in the darkest of times, there is always a glimmer of light on the horizon, a new beginning waiting to unfold.

And what a new beginning mine has been. With our development business behind us, Cyndi and I picked up and moved to Florida. Well, she went first, as she already had a job at a bank through a headhunter. I had a few house construction projects to finish, then followed. For 20 years, we had owned a beautiful investment home in Cape Coral. We'd rented it out on an annual basis for 19 years, and the tenant we had was a true gem—someone who treated the place like it was her own. When she was ready to move on, we knew it was time for us to move forward, too. Cyndi had already made the leap, moving down in April 2019 to start new opportunities. Meanwhile, I stayed behind in Rhode Island, taking care of the house we'd built and lived in for 22 years—our home on the water. There was cleaning to do, of course, but a couple of houses were still in the works for clients and some customer service tasks that needed to be wrapped up. Each day, I worked on getting the house ready for its sale, knowing this was the end of a chapter for us. It wasn't easy, but I found myself reflecting on all the years we'd spent there, all the memories tied to those walls. It was bittersweet.

Once Cyndi settled in Florida, I started making regular trips to see her. About once a month, I'd pack up and fly south, spending time with her while she built her new life. It wasn't until June 14th that we reached the point of no return. That's when we sold the house in Rhode Island, and I packed up the car for the long drive to Florida with my good friend Tim—another builder, now retired, and my partner in this new adventure.

Tim and I made a great team on the road—two old friends of 25 years, not in any rush, just enjoying the journey and the freedom that came with it. We stopped for coffee, talked about life, and laughed like we didn't have a care in the world. And really, at that moment, we didn't. In Florida, I transferred my Real Estate Broker's license and started working with a wonderful company there while testing to get my first captain's license. But something was different. I could feel the fatigue setting in, like an old pair of shoes that just weren't as comfortable anymore. After 37 years in the real estate business, I knew it was time to take a step back. The truth was, I was tired, and I could tell my patience wasn't what it used to be. It wasn't fair to anyone—my clients, my colleagues, or even myself—to keep going when my heart wasn't fully in it anymore. I worked my way through my 25ton, 50-ton, and eventually my 100-ton captain's licenses, earning well over the hours needed with my 40+ years of boating. I just needed the classes and tests, which took six months, but I still had the smaller license and could do taxis, tours, and teaching. At 58, after a long and fulfilling career, I realized it was time to let go. I'd had a good run— a great one—but I wasn't doing myself or anyone else any favors by continuing down a path that didn't feel right anymore. I needed to honor that feeling and make space for what was next. It wasn't about quitting but knowing when it was time to turn the page for the next chapter of my story.

There's a sense of peace that came with that decision, a sense of freedom that I hadn't realized I was craving. I'm excited for what's ahead, for the moments to be shared with Cyndi, and for the quiet satisfaction that comes with knowing I'm exactly where I'm supposed to be. There's a new rhythm to life here, and as I get used to it, I'm finding joy in the simple things—like sunshine on my face, the sound of the ocean in the distance, and the feeling that, no matter how long the journey has been, the next chapter is always waiting to be written.

Which isn't to say the past isn't a lovely place to visit. I often think about my sister Linda. Even now, it feels like she's just around the corner, as though I could pick up the phone and call her anytime. But it's been so long. Still, she's with me every single day. She was my little sister, and I was her big brother—two years older and full of mischief. I'll admit it: I showed her a few of the bad things we weren't supposed to do. In college, a little underage barhopping, some smoke, and sneaking off to beach bonfires were part of the "fun" we had. She was always game, and I was more than happy to lead the way. But of course, that big brother role wasn't all about the fun—it was about protecting her too, keeping an eye out, and making sure she knew she was loved, even when we were doing things we shouldn't.

It's funny how life comes full circle. Now, all these years later, I find myself in a similar position, watching over Linda's kids and loving them as my own. There are moments when I feel like I'm stepping into the big brother's role again, only this time, I'm not showing anyone how to sneak out of the house—I'm showing them how to live right. Sometimes I have to give a little verbal discipline in Linda's absence—just to make sure they remember their manners or remind them of the good values she taught them. And though it's a small thing, it feels important. These kids—Christopher, Connor, and Carly—are my heart, and I'm proud of who they've become. It's hard to believe that those mischievous little kids, full of energy and questions, are now grown with lives of their own.

Christopher and Connor, now 30, have turned into such strong, determined men. They're carving out careers and shaping their futures with the kind of dedication and drive I've always admired. Carly, their little sister, is 27, and she's just as impressive. I wish Linda could see them now—how they've grown into wonderful adults who contribute so much to the world. I know she'd be proud.

But it's not just about them. I can't talk about Linda's children without mentioning John, my brother-in-law. I've always known John was something special, but seeing him with my Sister's kids, it's clear just how much he's given to this family. He brought Linda's kids into their own, and together with Janet, John's wife of over 20 years, they've created something beautiful. With her gentle spirit and warm heart, Janet has been a steady and loving presence. The six of them—John, Janet, and their four adult children—have raised a family built on love, respect, and a deep sense of responsibility. It's a joy to see how well everyone has turned out. And of course, I can't forget Samantha, Janet's daughter, who's now 30 and turned into a wonderful woman. I love them all, and I'm so proud of the people they've become.

Over the years, I've also gotten to know and love my younger brother's family. We've been through a lot together— Linda's passing, Dad's passing, Mom's Alzheimer's. Tim, six years my junior, and his lovely wife, Michelle, have three beautiful daughters: Amanda, Emily, and Olivia. Those girls are my sunshine. Amanda is 26, Emily is 22, and Olivia is 17; each one is as unique and special as the next. I spoil them whenever I can—taking them out on my boat, bringing them to the beach, or just spending time with them in Florida, where life has taken us. Watching them grow into young women has been such a gift. They're smart, strong, and kind-hearted, and I can't wait to see the incredible things they'll do with their lives.

One thing I'm thankful for, above all else, is that, in our family, there's never bad blood, no arguments, no tension. We've always been able to come together with love and understanding, and that's something rare. I'm proud to be part of a family where everyone genuinely cares for each other and where the ties that bind us are stronger than any differences we might have.

I can't quite put into words the love I feel for my sister, her children, John, Janet, Samantha, and Tim's girls. It's a deep, abiding love that goes beyond the surface and into the very core of what family is all about. We're there for each other through thick and thin, which is what life is all about to me.

So, here's to the family that continues to grow and thrive, to the next generation, and to the memory of Linda, who taught me more than I could ever repay. I carry her with me every day, and I hope she can see how beautifully everything turned out, how loved her children are, and how much joy they continue to bring into my life.

Gregory, Uncle Ron, Christopher and Connor mimicking and making fun of the roadside statues in Martha's Vineyard.

*Linda 33, Myself 35, and Tim 29, at
Tim and Michelle's wedding 1997.*

*My nieces from brother and sisters-in-law. Amanda, Olivia,
Emily.*

3 great boating friends at a Big Brothers benefit 2001 (L) Gary, Myself and friend Tim.

Chris, Greg and Connor on our trip to the Vineyard

Wanda (real name Kristin), Steve, and Cyndi enjoying the Florida weather.

CHAPTER 10:
A NEW WAY TO MAKE A LIVING

Stepping back from my real estate career in my 50s, I found myself at a crossroads, unsure of what my next professional chapter would hold. We had enough money in the bank for retirement, and Cyndi had decided to continue working for a few more years, but I'd had it with the corporate world. All I knew was that I wanted, no, needed to do something that would keep me on the water and allow for the more relaxed lifestyle I craved after decades of grinding it out in the development business. "What you need is a retirement job," my wife Cyndi said with a knowing smile one evening as we sat on the back patio, watching the sun dip below the horizon. "Something to keep you out of trouble."

She was right, of course. Cyndi usually is about such things. My mind started whirring with possibilities. I couldn't picture myself spending my days on the golf course or parked in front of the TV. Boating has been my passion for as long as I can remember. What if I could find a way to make a living doing what I loved?

I got my six-pack captain's license first, and I worked at a small but successful company on the island of North Captiva. My job? Well, it was like being the island's personal chauffeur, but with a lot more salt water and a lot less formal wear. I ferried passengers to and from the island, took customers on leisurely lunch cruises, and—on the more adventurous days— played the role of the designated driver for drunken barhopping expeditions. And let's not forget the wildlife tours— taking people to see manatees and dolphins. But here's the real trick: you could make amazing tips if you could coax those dolphins into jumping over the wake behind the boat. There's nothing like the thrill of making a dolphin perform for a tip. Let me tell you, a showy dolphin is the key to a really good day at work. It was an odd but great gig—sunshine, sea air, and tips rolling in like the waves. You couldn't ask for much more.

That's when it hit me—boat delivery. Over the past 40 years, I've accrued thousands of hours on the water in all kinds of conditions, from glassy calm seas to raging nor'easters, and all just for friends, out of the kindness of my heart and the desire to be on the water. I wasn't getting paid for delivering my friends' boats, I didn't need one. I decided to get serious and work my way up from a six-pack captain's license to 25 tons, then 50 tons, and—just for fun—100 tons, all within six months. Why? Because, why not? It takes water hours and some bookwork, but I ended up with four times the hours needed to get these licenses. So now, I hold a 100-ton captain's license and feel as comfortable at the helm of an 80-foot yacht as I do behind the wheel of a car. I started putting out feelers, casually mentioning to friends and colleagues that I was available for deliveries should they ever need a hand. Before long, the phone began to ring. My first few gigs were low-key affairs—running a buddy's 35-foot Cabo to the Outer Banks, and helping another friend bring his new 43-foot Viking back from the Florida Keys. But the word quickly spread that Ron Smith was the guy to call when you needed your boat moved with a minimum of fuss and drama.

"You have a knack for this," my old pal Gary told me after a delivery. "The boat arrived in perfect condition, not a scratch on her. And you got her there faster than the owner could have done it himself." I realized then that there was a real need for experienced, reliable captains who could handle all kinds of vessels with skill and professionalism. Someone who would treat each boat as if it were their own, with an eye towards safety and efficiency. I began to think that maybe, just maybe, I had stumbled upon my next calling.

The more deliveries I made, the more I came to love the work. Every job presents its own unique challenges and learning opportunities. One week, I might be running a tricked-out 64-foot Hatteras with throttles that took a gentle hand; the next, a weather-beaten 34-foot Marine Trader that hadn't seen the business end of a sponge in years. I relished the variety, the constantly changing scenery, and the opportunity to pit my wits and skills against Mother Nature. I loved the work and never mind the long hours, even if that sometimes meant pulling a 24-hour overnight stint. But no matter how much I was enjoying the ride, I always knew to give the sea the respect, reverence, and dignity she deserved. After all, there's no arguing with her when you're out on the water. The wind doesn't care if you've got a schedule. The waves don't care if you need a nap. And the weather? Well, she's just waiting for you to get comfortable before throwing in a storm for fun.

Even in my 60s, I felt like a sponge, soaking up new knowledge at every turn. I learned the quirks and intricacies of different makes and models, the best anchorages to duck into when a squall blew up, and how to troubleshoot a faulty impeller at 2 a.m. with nothing but a Leatherman tool, duct tape, WD-40, and a flashlight. When deliveries called for additional crew, I took pride in showing the ropes to younger deckhands, many of whom had more enthusiasm than experience. I'd see their confidence grow with each trip as I taught them how to tie a proper cleat hitch, keep a lookout on a rolling sea, and trust their instincts and instruments in pea-soup fog.

Imparting the knowledge I'd spent a lifetime accumulating to the next generation felt enormously gratifying.

But it was more than just the actual boat handling that I found so fulfilling. The work scratched an itch I hadn't even fully realized I'd had—the need for constant movement, for seeking out new horizons. In between jobs, when I was back home for a few days, I'd find myself growing restless, scanning the weather reports and tide charts, eager for the next adventure.

Fortunately, Cyndi understood completely. She knew that boating was in my blood, as intrinsic to my being as the salt in my veins. The deliveries took me away from home for days or weeks at a stretch, but she never begrudged me for following my passion. "I'd rather have you out there doing what you love than putzing around here driving me crazy," she'd say with a wink when I called from some far-flung marina to check-in. "Just don't forget to come back to me."

As if I ever could. Cyndi remained my anchor, the force that tethered me to land even as my heart belonged to the sea. She understood me in a way that no one else quite could.

That's not to say the work was easy by any stretch. The hours could be long and grueling, with pre-dawn departures, and overnight spent toiling at the helm, aching muscles from constant boat-schlepping. I quickly learned to catch sleep in snatches, to subsist on lukewarm coffee and Clif bars, and to make peace with my own company during long, lonely stretches offshore.

Every delivery had its share of minor crises that tested my problem-solving abilities. A chafed fan belt that needed MacGyvering. A busted bilge pump that demanded bailing by hand. An amperage drop that left us limping towards shore on one engine, watching the depth sounder while holding my breath. But that was part of the gig—expecting the unexpected, relying on your wits and experience to see you through safely to the other side.

There were moments of sheer terror, like the time a rogue wave nearly pitch-poled the 60-foot Azimut I was delivering up the coast in an unexpected storm. And moments of transcendent beauty, like watching the moon rise over an endless expanse of silver-limned sea, the boat's wake unfurling behind us like a satin ribbon. In those instances, I felt a bone-deep connectedness to something larger than myself, a sense of my own tiny place in the grand tapestry. No, the work wasn't always a picnic. But it was never dull. And it brought me more satisfaction than anything I'd done in years. With each delivery, I felt the old thrum of excitement, the zesty tingle of something new. I'd found my niche, my purpose, and I intended to squeeze every drop out of it.

My little boat delivery side hustle blossomed into a full-fledged business as word got around. Inquiries flooded in from up and down the eastern seaboard. Before long, I was booking jobs months in advance, toggling between hurricanes to avoid weather delays, and puzzling out logistics like a master conductor.

Some of the boats that passed through my hands were real beauties—sleek, lovingly-maintained thoroughbreds that all but leaped over the waves. Others were more akin to twenty mules, stolid and dependable but hardly the stuff of nautical centerfolds. I came to love them all for their quirks and personalities. Much like dogs, boats have souls, I've always maintained. You just must learn how to listen to them.

As my reputation grew, so did the profile of my clients. I started getting calls from business tycoons lured by word of mouth and the promise of discretion. I ferried gleaming 80-foot San Lorenzo's, fast 60-foot Sunseekers, 55-foot Vikings, and Predators that cost more than most houses—even moved a totally restored 1970s Bertram Motor yacht—always mindful of the awesome responsibility that had been placed in my hands. There was no room for error when a single nick in the teak decking could mean thousands of dollars for repairs. But I found that I thrived under pressure. The higher the stakes, the more focused and clear-headed I became. Nothing rattled me, not engine failures, inexperienced deckhands, or even the occasional on-board meltdown. I'd seen it all and then some.

As I reflect on it now, it all feels so inevitable, like an arrow loose from a bow. Boating has been a great love and defining force of my life in many ways—as recreation, an escape, solace and joy, and adrenaline-fueled thrill. I've owned 14 boats in my lifetime, each different from the other because they all operate and handle differently. It only makes sense that it became my livelihood as well as how I help support myself and my family.

When I plan to retire, people sometimes ask me to hang up my captain's hat and retreat to a condo somewhere. I just smile and shake my head. Life on the water isn't a pastime or even a vocation. It's a calling, as vital and necessary as the breath in my lungs. I can't imagine my existence without the slap of waves against the hull, the tang of salt air in my nose, the delicate dance of wind and current and tide. Commanding a vessel—no matter how large or small— flexes every muscle and all my mental faculties. It demands fortitude, ingenuity, and resilience. In short, it makes me feel alive.

So, I'll keep doing this work for as long as the sea will have me, for as long as my body and mind can. I know it won't be forever. There will come a day when I make my last trip, when I give my final benediction to Neptune and point my bow toward home. When that happens, I hope I'll be able to look back and say that I fully leveraged the adventure and challenge of this salty life and that I took the great gift I was given—this abiding love for the open water—and transformed it into something meaningful. A way to touch other lives, to forge connections, to pass along the precious cargo of experience from one generation to the next.

For now, I'm content with what I've built, with the niche I've carved. Each boat delivery, each lesson imparted, and each nautical map annotated feels like a small, vital link in the long chain of my aquatic life. A reminder that I'm a part of something larger than myself, a continuum that stretches back to the first humans who lashed logs together and shoved off from shore in search of new frontiers. "And you call yourself retired," Cyndi teases when I come home, windburned and bone-weary, after a particularly grueling trip. She's curled up on the couch, flipping through a magazine, the very picture of domestic bliss.

"I'm a lucky man," I tell her, and I mean it from the soles of my Topsiders to the tip of my hat. She arches a knowing eyebrow.

"Oh, I'm well aware. But I bet you'll be chomping at the bit to get back out there in approximately 48 hours."

She's wrong—I give it 36 hours, tops. But as I sink down next to her, breathing in the familiar smells of home, I feel competing urges to stay put and to shove off, warring within me. The yin and yang of a life in constant motion.

It's a tension I've come to accept, even to be grateful for. Because I've been able to alchemize my passion into a new way of making my way in the world, long after I thought I'd charted all my possible courses. And for that, I consider myself the richest of men.

Mother and baby dolphins playing in the wake of my boat.

The elusive "Green Flash"— when conditions are perfect on a sunset, there can be a flash of green just as the sun sets.

Beautiful moon flickering on the nighttime water.

CHAPTER 11:
SEAFARING FRIENDS AND COMFORT FOODS

When you spend as much time on the water as I have, you quickly learn that there are two essential ingredients to any successful voyage: good companions and good grub. And over the years, I've been lucky enough to have plenty of both.

Let's start with the companions. Now, I've had my share of salty dogs on board—crusty old sailors with more stories than teeth and egos to match. But the best shipmate I ever had was a little guy named Prince, who never said a word but always knew what I needed.

Prince was my Shih Tzu I bought 5 years before Cyndi walked back into my life, and he took to boating like a duck to water (well, except for the actual water part—more on that later). From the moment I brought him home as a pup, he was my constant companion on every voyage, from lazy afternoon cruises to multi-day deliveries up and down the coast.

He had his own designated seat on every boat I owned, right next to the helm, where he could keep an eye on things. And let me tell you, that little furball was better than any GPS when it came to navigation. He seemed to have a sixth sense for when something wasn't quite right, whether it was a change in the engine pitch or an unexpected shift in the wind.

But Prince really shone in his ability to attract attention from the fairer sex, when I was single, of course. I swear, that dog was better than any wingman I ever had. All he had to do was sit there looking cute (which, let's be honest, was his default state), and women would come flocking from all corners of the marina.

"Oh, my goodness, look at that adorable little face!" they'd coo, bending down to scratch him behind the ears. "What's his name?"

"Prince," I'd reply with a grin, knowing full well that I had them hooked. "But you can call me Captain Ron."

It was a foolproof system, and it never failed to amaze me how a 10-pound ball of fluff could be such an effective chick magnet. Of course, it probably didn't hurt that I was a tall, tanned, and (if I do say so myself) devilishly handsome sailor with a twinkle in my eye and a knack for spinning a good yarn. But still, I had to give credit where credit was due.

There was just one small problem with Prince's love of boating: he hated the actual water with passion. I mean, this dog would do anything to avoid getting his paws wet. He'd balance on the gunnels of the boat with the grace of a tightrope walker, or leap from seat to seat like a furry little parkour artist, just to avoid a splash.

One time, we were out on a particularly choppy day, and a wave broke over the bow, soaking Prince from head to tail. The poor little guy let out a yelp and scrambled up my leg like a squirrel up a tree, clinging to my neck for dear life. From that day on, he made sure to stay well clear of the edges of the boat, no matter how calm the seas were.

But despite his hydrophobia, Prince was the best first mate a captain could ask for. He was always ready with a wag of the tail and a snuggle when I needed it most, and he never complained about the long hours or the cramped quarters. In fact, I'm pretty sure he thought he was living the high life, getting to spend all day with his favorite human and a never-ending supply of salty snacks. He's now in dog heaven, waiting for me to join him when the time comes.

Of course, Prince wasn't my only companion on these voyages. Over the years, I've had the pleasure of working with some truly talented and dedicated crew members, none more so than my friend Corey.

Now, when I first agreed to take on a new deckhand for a delivery job, I must admit I was a little skeptical. I'd had my share of greenhorns over the years and knew how much work it could be to train someone up from scratch. But the owner of this boat insisted that this Corey character was the real deal—a skilled sailor with a 25-ton license, a solid work ethic, and a can-do attitude.

So, imagine my surprise when, on the morning of our departure, a petite blonde woman strolled up the dock with a duffel bag slung over her shoulder and a big grin on her face. "Captain Ron?" she called out, sticking out her hand for a shake. "I'm Corey. Ready to set sail?"

I was a little taken aback at first. In all my years of boating, I'd never worked with a female deckhand before. But as soon as we got underway, it became clear that Corey knew her stuff. She could tie a bowline faster than most guys I knew, was very good with charts and the GPS, and had a knack for anticipating what needed to be done before I even had to ask.

Over the course of that first trip, Corey and I fell into an easy rhythm, working together like a well-oiled machine. We'd trade off watches at the helm, swap stories over cups of strong coffee, and even belt out the occasional sea-shanty when the mood struck (although, honestly, neither of us was blessed with a great singing voice).

As the miles flew by and the coastline rolled past, I found myself growing more and more impressed with Corey's skills and dedication. She was a natural-born sailor with a deep love and respect for the sea that rivaled my own. And when the going got tough—as it inevitably does on any long voyage —she never once complained or lost her cool, although there may have been an occasional "shit, damn, or f**k" tossed into the air if the boat wasn't cooperating. That's part of being on the sea. I remember one particularly hairy moment, when we were caught in a sudden squall off the coast of Cape Hatteras. The wind was howling, the rain was coming down in sheets, and visibility was practically zero. But Corey never flinched. She just calmly went about her duties, manning the helm like a pro.

When the storm finally passed, and we emerged into the sun on the other side, I couldn't help but feel a swell of pride for my plucky first mate. "Nice work back there," I told her, clapping her on the shoulder. "You're a hell of a sailor, Corey."

She just grinned and shrugged, like it was no big deal. "Just doing my job, Cap," she said. "Besides, I learned from the best."

From that moment on, Corey became my go-to deckhand for any delivery job. We'd done dozens of trips together, from Maine to Miami, the Bahamas, and everywhere in between. And no matter what the weather or the boat threw at us, I knew I could always count on her to have my back.

But Corey was just one of the many colorful characters I've had the pleasure of working with over the years.

Unfortunately, Corey left our team at the end of the summer of '24 to pursue delivering sailboats. It is an area I have yet to attempt, except by motoring, but she loved the sailing experience, and I'm sure she will be very good at it.

There were also people like my friends Gary and Sharon, the entrepreneurial couple who bought a 43-foot trawler and set off to cruise the Bahamas, the US coast, and the Caribbean upon retiring. I remember helping them bring their boat up from Florida to Rhode Island, where they were planning to spend the summer before heading south again in the fall. Gary was a born tinkerer, always fiddling with some piece of equipment or another, while Sharon was the epitome of grace under pressure, keeping everyone fed and happy no matter what the conditions.

Watching the two of them banter back and forth, it was clear that they had the kind of easy, comfortable relationship that only came from years of partnership and shared adventures. As we made our way up the coast, stopping in quaint little towns along the way for provisions and sightseeing, I could see the excitement and anticipation building in their eyes.

Sharon couldn't resist buying a few jars of locally made jam to take with them on their travels.

"For when we're on the islands and missing a taste of home," she explained with a wistful smile.

As we said our goodbyes at the end of the trip, I couldn't help but feel a pang of envy for the adventure that lay ahead of them. But at the same time, I knew that I had my own adventures waiting for me—new horizons to explore and new friends to make along the way.

For friends like Glen and Donna, I helped them bring their 32-foot Ocean Sportfish (a pocket rocket) down from Maine to Newport for summertime fun and offshore exploring. Glenn came on many canyon runs for tuna with me. And then there was Tony and Flora. They were a little longer in the tooth but still behaved like 40-year-old kids. Tony was a master storyteller, always ready with a joke or a tall tale to keep us entertained on the long watches. And Flora, a galley wizard, whipped up gourmet meals from the most basic ingredients. I swear, that woman could make a five-star dinner out of a can of tuna and a handful of stale crackers. Now, that wasn't all Flora was good for. She was an open ear, always ready to listen and offer advice. She was also a huge instigator who could make people party even harder with her famous Fireball shots. But what I remember most about the trip with Glenn and Mike was the sense of camaraderie and shared purpose that developed between the three of us. We were all chasing the same dream, in our own ways—the freedom and adventure of the open sea, the chance to see the world on our own terms.

As we made our way down the coast, stopping in places like Plymouth, where we tied up just a stone's throw from the famous rock, seeing the whales off Boston Harbor, and experiencing the majesty of going through the Cape Cod Canal, where the intercostal starts its over 3000-mile run to Brownsville, Texas, I couldn't help but feel a deep sense of gratitude for the life I'd chosen.

Because really, when you get right down to it, that's what boating is all about—the people you meet, the experiences you share, the memories you make along the way. And, of course, the food.

Oh, the food. If there's one thing I've learned in all my years of being on the water, it's that good eats are the key to a happy crew. And over the years, I've had the pleasure of sampling some of the finest local specialties that the coastal towns of America have to offer.

Down in the Carolinas, it's all about hush puppies, shrimp, and barbecue. I remember, with Corey, tying up in a little town called Calabash, where the main drag was lined with seafood shacks all vying for the title of the best seafood in town. The World War II years saw Calabash opening restaurants and serving seafood cooked with a special flavor. This was the birth of "Calabash Seafood." A few years later, Calabash would become known as "The Seafood Capital of the World." We must have sampled half a dozen different places before settling on a little hole-in-the-wall joint called the Boundary House.

The shrimp were as big as my fist, lightly battered and fried to a golden crisp. And the hush puppies—oh man, those hush puppies. Fluffy on the inside, crunchy on the outside, with just a hint of sweetness from the cornmeal. We ate until we were fit to burst, washing it all down with ice-cold sweet tea and locally brewed beer.

Tybee Island, Georgia. Bubba Gumbo's had the best gumbo I've ever tasted. It's right there in the name, and boy, it delivers on flavor. Further up the coast in Maryland, it's all about the crab. One summer, I tied up in Annapolis and found Cantler's Riverside Inn packed with locals and tourists at communal tables. We ordered steamed blue crabs, and after a quick lesson on how to crack them open, we spent hours picking away at the sweet meat, swapping stories, and feeling like we'd uncovered a local treasure.

Not all my culinary adventures were upscale, though. In a small New Jersey town, I happened upon Dominick's, an old Italian joint with faded Formica tables and a battered jukebox. The spaghetti and meatballs were a revelation—rich sauce, giant meatballs, and ginger ale served in juice glasses. We left content, reflecting on life's simple pleasures on the water.

The challenges of life at sea—long hours and unpredictable weather—were outweighed by moments of joy: a perfect docking, a well-cooked meal shared, and the tranquility of night watch under the moon and stars. Each day brought new adventures, from playful dolphins, hidden coves, and new friends.

This sense of adventure fuels my return to the water, pushing me beyond my comfort zone. Through my journey, I've formed deep friendships and experienced endless gratitude for the life I've led and enjoyed so far. The sea has been my teacher and muse, granting me purpose and passion.

Prince walking the docks in Newport letting everyone know who's the boss of the marina.

Great friends boating and all around, Gary and Sharon.

Prince in heaven running to meet me when it's my time.

CHAPTER 12:
ADVENTURES IN BOATING

My seafaring adventures have taken me up and down the eastern seaboard as far inland as the Great Lakes on various sizes of boats with different crew members. I could fill more books with my boating stories, but here's a snapshot.

Newport

Ah, Newport. What a charming, historic place. The foundations of the buildings are made of rock, dating back hundreds of years to simpler times. But navigating the waters around Newport is anything but simple, especially if you're unlucky enough to catch the tide going out. Billions of gallons of water squeeze through narrow passages, trying to escape Narragansett Bay, while you're fighting to get in. The waves rear up, six to seven feet high, tossing your boat around like a rubber ducky in a Jacuzzi.

And the cost of docking in Newport? Don't even get me started. Let's just say it's not for the faint of heart or light of wallet. But hey, that's the price you pay for a slice of boating paradise.

Tampa Bay

Speaking of paradise, there's nothing quite like a leisurely two-day trip in a sailboat puttering along at five knots with a little 9.9 horsepower engine. Sure, the big boats zoom by impatiently as you chug through the drawbridges and shipping channels. But who cares? You've got porpoises playfully swimming around in the summer, harbor seals in the winter and spring, and an open horizon ahead no matter the season.

Intracoastal – St. Augustine to Newport, R.I.

The Intracoastal is not always smooth sailing, even on a trusty 48-foot Sea Ray—a great boat for island-hopping, but perhaps not entirely cut out for the high seas. Corey and I quickly discovered this while attempting to navigate the southern Intracoastal waters. As we drifted along, snacking on boiled peanuts and "mud bugs" (crawdads taste far better than they sound), an eerie mist began to descend. I glanced around, suddenly realizing we were the only boat in sight. An uneasy feeling crept over me. Were we lost? Off course? I tried to shake it off, but Corey looked positively green, and not just from the mudbugs. While Corey is an excellent first mate in most regards, she harbors an unshakable phobia of docking larger boats. So here I was, fog closing in, compass spinning uselessly, with a jittery docking-phobic mate. Perfect.

Blanketed in the eerie, impenetrable mist, I slowed the boat to a crawl, my eyes straining to pick out the blinking green and red of the channel markers. The radar showed a smattering of other vessels nearby, but it was impossible to tell what direction they were heading or how fast they were moving.

I thought back to my early days of boating, before GPS and chart plotters and all the other technological marvels that have made navigation so much easier. Back then, you relied on your wits and instincts, on the subtle cues from the wind and the water. You developed a sixth sense for when something wasn't quite right, a prickly feeling at the base of your spine that told you to pay attention.

Back in the '70s and '80s, we didn't have GPS or smartphones—just a chart, a compass, a depth finder, and our wits. Fog? Oh, it wasn't the soft, spooky kind you get in Florida. It was the thick, roll-up-your-sleeves kind you find in New England, where you couldn't see 25 feet in front of you. And trust me, that fog loved to turn you around without asking. You'd think you were going straight, but surprise!—you were heading in the complete opposite direction.

Enter the compass. In those days, it was the only thing that kept us from sailing into the abyss or a rock (usually a rock). GPS came along in the early '90s, but it had a little "quirk"---it was off by 300 yards because, apparently, the military didn't trust foreign military powers or even us with perfect accuracy. I spent $2300 on a GPS the size of a shoebox, and all it did was give me Lat/Long coordinates. So, I'd write those onto a paper chart and pray we didn't crash into a buoy. Sure, it was a huge improvement over getting lost in the fog, but it wasn't exactly easy. And the VHF radio? That was the only way to call for help, not a cellphone---because remember, we weren't texting selfies, we were just hoping not to hit rocks.

In the end, you trusted your compass, your depth finder, and maybe a prayer or two. The sea might trick you, but hey, at least we were never bored!

That familiar feeling of being out of my depth rushed back as I navigated the Sea Ray through the fog. Expecting a foghorn, I instead heard only the engine's thrum and water slapping against the hull.

Georgia – 42-foot catamaran

And then, in Georgia, came the horseflies. Not just a few pesky swarms, but a full-on Biblical plague of them, coating every surface of the boat. Poor Corey—armed with only a flimsy flyswatter, she did her best Rambo impression, determinedly smacking at the relentless buggers. I swear we must have killed hundreds, but they just kept coming from the salt marsh swamps and sawgrass of this part of the intercostal, like some bad Hitchcock film. My dreams of a peaceful, picturesque journey quickly morphed into a buzzing, biting, floating nightmare. But hey, if you can't beat 'em, join 'em, right? So, Corey and I made a little game of it, keeping score of our horsefly "hits" — 10 points for the fat ones, five points for the quicker buggers. Suddenly, it didn't seem so bad; the dread of docking dimmed in comparison to the satisfaction of nailing a juicy fly right between its beady little eyes.

Yet all the horsefly hunting in the world couldn't have prepared us for Mother Nature's next surprise. We were off Palm Beach, making our way out of a channel and into the open ocean. We endured rough three-to-five-foot seas, which rocked the sailboat, and I don't sail. So, we were under the power of two Yanmar diesels, prepared to do a few 24-hour stints. The trip to Marathon was long with the sea hitting us broadside. We were exhausted from battle, and nighttime was falling, when suddenly--- wham! Something slammed into the hull of our 42-foot catamaran. Then again—thud! And again. Corey and I looked at each other in bewilderment and slight trepidation. Were we under attack? Had the horseflies called in reinforcements? Hearts pounding, we cautiously made our way to the bow, ready to confront our assailants...only to find a school of flying fish, smacking mindlessly into our ship as they tried to evade some predator below–probably a sailfish. Crisis averted, we couldn't help but laugh at ourselves and the absurdity of our high-seas adventures.

Because that's the thing about boating—you never know what you're going to encounter out there. Whether it's battling Biblical bug plagues, getting lost in the mist, or facing down mysterious underwater creatures, every day is a new escapade. But that's what keeps us going back for more. That tantalizing promise that you never know what lies ahead. As long as we've got a sturdy hull beneath us, a sense of humor to keep us afloat, and a healthy dose of Dramamine, we'll keep riding the waves and seeking out new thrills. The tides may change, but the lure of the sea remains as strong as ever, calling us onward to our next great boating adventure. And I've had my fair share of seafaring adventures.

Florida - 21-foot speedboat, Quicksilver

When I finally moved back from Florida, I couldn't wait to get a boat. I had friends with boats, sure, but I needed my own. I mean,

I'm a guy who calls the water home. So, when my neighbor mentioned he was selling his 21-foot Wellcraft speedboat, I thought, "Why not? Let's test it out!" I took it for a spin, and naturally, I was hooked. I immediately bought it, named her Quicksilver (because, you know, it's fast, or at least it sounded fast), and parked her on a dock. Life was good, except for the little detail that, at 6'4", I was way too tall for the boat's sleeping quarters.

Quicksilver now had this tiny cabin, or as I called it, a glorified closet with cushions. The space was meant for two people side by side, but let's be real—only if they were both hobbits. The bed was only six feet long, and the port-a-potty? Yeah, it was cleverly hidden under the cushions, which was great unless you or your bedmate needed to use it in the middle of the night. Picture this: you're sleeping like a baby, then suddenly, someone has to get up and go. They'd shake you awake, ask you to move, pull up the cushions, and hop out of bed like you're in a weird, cramped game of musical chairs. And, of course, no air conditioning—just the door wide open and morning dew soaking into your feet. It was the height of luxury, I tell you.

But hey, Quicksilver was good to me for a few years. We had some fun times but a few harrowing ones too, especially when the seas were a little rough for such a small boat. Sleeping on Block

Island? Let's just say it felt like being trapped in a sausage casing but with more saltwater and less dignity.

Eventually, I sold her to an engineer from Barrington and thought, "That's it. Quicksilver has sailed into the sunset." Well, apparently not. One evening, I heard she caught fire and burned right down to the waterline. Guess that's one way to go out in style. Fire is probably the only thing that could make Quicksilver faster than she ever was on the water!

Point Judith to Martha's Vineyard to Falmouth to Point Judith - 26-foot Sea Ray.

Another weekend, I took my good friend Fran to Martha's Vineyard for a four-day getaway on my 26-foot Sea Ray. We had a blast hitting up the local clubs, checking out the sights, and enjoying the beach. But, as you know, Jaws is never far from my mind whenever I go near the ocean. The Vineyard was where they filmed much of that movie, and I'm a bit shark-averse. Not to mention, there's a healthy population of them just 60 miles away in Chatham on Cape Cod.

On Sunday, we decided to head back to Point Judith, but the weather had other plans. We got about 20 miles out to Cuttyhunk when, out of nowhere—bam—the calm seas turned into six-foot waves. The rain came sideways, lightning crackled around us, and I could practically hear the sharks laughing in the distance. Now, I'll brave high seas, pelting rain, and thunder all day, but lightning? Nope. No, thank you. I was not sticking around to become a human lightning rod.

We turned around faster than a boat with a rocket attached to it. There was no time to cover the cockpit, so I floored the 454 engine and headed for the nearest marina in Falmouth, which, coincidentally, is where Dr. Robert Ballard, the guy who found the Titanic, operates from. I couldn't see a thing through the sideways rain; the engine was screaming like it was auditioning for a horror movie, and the sky was putting on a light show we didn't ask for.

Finally, we reached Woods Hole in Falmouth but couldn't find a dock, so I did the next best thing: I jumped out onto the smooth rock seawall and tied the boat to two trees. Yes, trees. Because why not? We threw the canvas top over, got into dry clothes, and waited out the storm. Once it passed, the sky cleared, the seas calmed, and we cruised back home to Point Judith under bright, sunny skies—three-foot seas, no wind, just a peaceful ride. Of course, I like to think the sharks took one look at us and thought, "Eh, they're fine. Let them be."

Maine to Plymouth Rock to Point Judith – 32-foot powerboat

One time, Mike, Glenn, the owner, and I set out to deliver a 32-foot Ocean powerboat from Kennebunkport, Maine, to Point Judith. It was a fantastic boat, which I lovingly called the "pocket rocket." Despite its size, it had an "Ocean" hull and could hold its own. Now, Maine in the fog? Yeah, that's something else. As we left the Kennebunk River, visibility was so bad it felt like we were in the middle of a ghost story—25 to 100 feet of fog everywhere. We took it slowly at first, navigating around granite outcroppings we couldn't even see until we were practically on top of them. It was like driving blindfolded with the occasional "Whoops! Almost hit that!" shout.

But then, as luck would have it, the fog finally lifted, and we were able to get a good five to 10 miles offshore and cruise south. That's when the magic happened---whales. We started seeing them popping up like they were trying to steal the show. You know, the kind of whales that make you feel like you're in a nature documentary, and they're putting on a special performance just for you. We spent a good amount of time watching them frolic because, honestly, when's the last time you saw a whale, right? At this point, we were both feeling proud of ourselves, like we were some kind of whale-watching experts.

After a while, we decided it was time to head to Plymouth, Massachusetts, for the night. We were docked right next to Plymouth Rock, the legendary spot where the Pilgrims are supposed to have landed. I had this grand vision of a massive, awe-inspiring rock—something so impressive that it would make you believe the whole founding of America thing was set in stone, right? Well, let me tell you, Plymouth Rock is not the towering monolith you imagine. It's a modest little slab about five feet by three feet, surrounded by a cage like it's some kind of rock zoo exhibit. I mean, we all stood there, looking at it, and then looked at each other like, "Wait... that's it?" I was half-expecting a tour guide to jump out and say, "And here, we have the world's most famous small rock, folks! Enjoy!" Very underwhelming.

The next morning, we made our way toward the Cape Cod Canal, the shortcut that cuts across Massachusetts. This is the main shipping channel, which means you must dodge tugboats, barges, and, of course, the notorious current. That current runs at about 6 knots and changes direction every six hours. So, naturally, we got stuck in the worst of it. Despite cruising at 25 knots on the boat, we were barely making 20 knots over the ground because the tide was working against us. It was like trying to sprint on a treadmill that's set to a faster pace than you can handle. At one point, Mike looked at me and said, "At this rate, we could probably just walk the boat through the canal faster!"

After passing through the canal and emerging into Buzzards Bay, a fierce wind nearly knocked us off course. I throttled back, trying to maintain control as the boat bucked and heaved, dishes clattering in the galley. With no turning back, I steered into each wave, determined to prove my seamanship against nature's fury.

Hours blurred as the rough sea tested my endurance. Finally, the wind eased, and the waves smoothed out. We had weathered the worst—battered but unbroken.

And we did all of this in the "pocket rocket," a boat that could've easily outrun a lot of things if the tides weren't laughing at us. But hey, we made it through, and we lived to tell the tale. Plymouth Rock may have disappointed us, but the adventure? It was worth the price of admission.

Florida to New York – 80-foot yacht

On another one of my adventures, I got a call on short notice to co-captain an 80-foot San Lorenzo yacht. The destination was a

Brooklyn, New York marina, looking across the water from Manhattan. The original co-captain couldn't make it, and I was given one day's notice to pack my bags, drive across Alligator Alley to West Palm Beach, and meet the crew. I was in—who wouldn't jump at the chance to captain an 80-foot yacht?

I met the first mate, who was from Venezuela and spoke very little English (he usually worked on larger transport ships, so he wasn't used to the luxury yacht gig). We spent the night at the marina, and the next day, we topped off the diesel tanks and set off. The weather was smooth, the seas calm, and there were turtles lazily swimming in the Gulf Stream while dolphins played in our wake. "Red sky at night, sailors' delight," I thought, feeling all kinds of confidence. This was going to be an easy, breezy trip.

The first leg of the journey was smooth. We watched the sunset and sailed through the night. We hit St. Augustine early in the morning. The plan was to top off the fuel and meet the other captain's family for lunch. The second leg was supposed to be a straight 24-hour shot to the Outer Banks. No big deal, right? But, as luck would have it, we were about 80 miles offshore when all hell broke loose. A squall hit us like a freight train—eight-to-10-foot seas and winds up to 50 miles per hour. The boat was tossing like a salad, and we didn't have the fancy stabilizers that most boats this size must have to smooth things out. Suddenly, the salon looked like a scene from a disaster movie. Drawers flew open, cabinets exploded, and everything that wasn't nailed down turned into a projectile. Vacuum cleaners, buckets, and TV remotes were all flying around like they were auditioning for Tornado: The Sequel.

Now, I've never been one to get seasick. I love being on the water, and nothing makes me happier than a good, bumpy ride. But I'll admit—when I saw the deckhand on the outside deck, clutching the rails while getting pelted with rain and vomiting overboard, I realized this might not be your average boat trip. Meanwhile, I was running around the salon, trying to secure things before they were smashed. First, I used a whole roll of blue painter's tape (I had never felt more like a handyman in my life), but when that didn't hold, it was time to break out the big guns—duct tape. The boat tossed me around like a ragdoll, and every time I tried to tape something down, I'd get thrown across the boat to the couch. At least the couch was secure!

In the chaos, I managed to tape down drawers, cabinets, lamps, and anything that would've shattered in the storm. By some miracle, NOTHING broke. I can only assume that duct tape and sheer willpower were holding that boat together. After what felt like an eternity, the storm cleared as suddenly as it had arrived—30 minutes of chaos, then nothing.

But, of course, just as things seemed to settle down, we hit another snag. The starboard transmission wouldn't engage. Oh, of course it wouldn't. We were now 60 miles off Hilton Head with only one working engine. At this point, I couldn't even blame the storm. We turned west and limped into Hilton Head at a meager 12 knots, arriving around 6 p.m.

The next morning, a mechanic came aboard and found the problem—it turns out, the clutch plate was fried, but it wasn't anything too serious. However, the mechanic was three weeks out for parts, and there were boats in front of us. The owner decided to cut the trip short, as it was already July, and half the summer was gone. So, the other captain stayed with the boat and the mate, and I got a flight home.

The yacht was fixed and turned around, but not before I had one last laugh. You know, when your boat turns into a

DIY project of duct tape, painter's tape, and praying to the sea gods, it's hard not to chuckle at the absurdity of it all. Sometimes, adventure is more about the things that don't go right. And if nothing else, I learned that a little tape and a lot of patience can get you through just about anything, even an 80-foot yacht ride from hell.

Honestly, it was my most adventurous journey yet, and I wouldn't trade a minute of it. Would I do it again? Probably not. Would I tell the story over and over? Oh, absolutely. And if I'm being honest, I still think the real lesson I learned is that if you're ever in doubt, always pack extra duct tape.

Detroit to New York to Point Judith - 44-foot Post Sportfisher

For 13 glorious years, I owned a 44-foot Post Sportfisher called Relentless, and let me tell you, she was relentless in every sense of the word. This boat could power through eight-foot seas like they were speed bumps and never once slowed down. Whether we were offshore chasing tuna in the Gulf Stream or navigating some pretty dicey waters, she was the boat you wanted to be on if you were going to make it home safely.

Now, the Gulf Stream is a magical place—literally a highway for big predators. Bluefin tuna, yellowfin, Mahi, sharks, whales, you name it. The temperature jumps 15-20 degrees, and suddenly, you're cruising through waters that feel like summer, even if you leave the dock at 3 a.m. in a brisk 55-degree chill. But once you hit the edge of the canyon, it's like flipping a switch—depths drop from 300 to 1,500 feet in no time, and everything comes alive. It's like the ocean is giving you a VIP pass to its wildest party.

But before I got to enjoy all that glory, I had to get Relentless from Detroit to Rhode Island. Which, of course, was not without incident. I bought the boat as a repo, and it took me 10 days to bring her home. Four of those days? Spent in the Erie Canal. Yeah, the Great Lakes are fun, but when you're trying to get a 44-footer through the locks, you really appreciate the phrase "smooth sailing" in a whole new way. On Day One, we had a hose spring a leak, which is fine, except the first fix involved duct tape. Classic. I'm pretty sure duct tape is the unofficial sponsor of every boating adventure, right?

We hit a few more snags, but eventually, we were on the Hudson River, just north of Albany, enjoying a nice steak dinner at a local spot. And that's when we decided to do what every fine, upstanding group of boaters does: naturally visit a gentlemen's club. But here's the kicker—no alcohol was served at the club! So, you had to buy your drinks next door, then bring them over to the club. Honestly, I have no idea what I was expecting, but I can tell you it wasn't that. We left with more questions than answers, but it was an adventure.

Then came the bridges. As we headed south, the outriggers had to come down to fit under the overpasses of the 35 locks of the Erie Canal, but we didn't consider that they were still 34 feet tall. We came to the Bridge on the Hudson and stopped dead in our tracks. The Green Island Bridge? It was 32 feet above the water. So, there we were, in a full-blown outboard-engineering crisis, trying to figure out how to get under it. Genius plan? Well, we decided to bend the fiberglass poles. Yeah, you heard that right. The guys hung off the outrigger ropes and literally bent the poles until they scraped under the bridge. I swear, we made it by inches. I'm still not sure how we didn't lose our balance and fall into the river.

But we survived, and after a few laughs, the rest of the trip went smoothly. We cruised past landmarks like Bannerman Castle (a Revolutionary War relic), under the George Washington Bridge, and around the Statue of Liberty, which really made you feel good about being an American. The Twin Towers were still standing back then, so I could see them from the boat. A humbling sight, for sure.

Now, as much fun as it was to go up the East River, through the treacherous currents of Hell's Gate, past Rikers Island, and then full steam into Long Island Sound, what really got my heart racing was the infamous "Race"—a swift stretch of water between Fishers

Island and Long Island, where even submarines must make sure no one's around. Coast Guard boats with 50-caliber guns pointed at you while you're just trying to enjoy a nice ride? That's an adrenaline rush I can't quite explain.

But after all the adventures, the boats, the locks, and the duct tape, the one thing I learned for sure is this: When you're on a boat like Relentless, you better be ready for anything. Especially when you're 60 miles off the coast and suddenly realize the only thing you really need to survive is a whole lot of duct tape, a good crew, and the ability to laugh at all the chaos that comes with it.

Florida to Rhode Island - 48-foot yacht

It was a crisp, early morning when we set off from Stuart, Florida, aboard a 48-foot yacht. The air was fresh, the sun was rising, and everything felt like the beginning of an epic adventure. And it would be—just not the way I'd imagined.

Corey, my trusty first mate, never really liked docking or undocking bigger boats. She was excellent with the 20 to 30-footers she worked on around Tampa Bay, but when it came to our 48-footer, she'd turn the helm over to me, every single time.

The water was flat and calm as we hit the open ocean at around 7 a.m.. Dolphins darted around us like they were auditioning for a marine-themed reality show. We were cruising along about five miles offshore, passing Melbourne and Merritt Island, when the iconic sight of Cape Canaveral appeared in the distance, with its rocket launch pads giving me chills. There's nothing quite like the sight of industrial rocket launchers when you're just trying to get to the next marina.

And then, it happened. We crossed New Smyrna Beach and encountered this rebuilt wooden yacht—about 50 feet long, all rebuilt and beautiful, looking like something from a James Bond movie. Fast. Very fast. It zipped past us with ease, leaving us in its wake, and I couldn't help but feel a little envious. It reminded me of the International Yacht Restoration School boats in Newport, Rhode Island. I turned to Corey and said, "Imagine what we could do with that kind of speed."

Her response? "Yeah, but then I'd have to dock it."

Fast forward a few hours, and we're in the channel heading into New Smyrna Beach. Everything was going well until the port engine decided to shut down. It was like the yacht had suddenly entered protest mode. "Oh, you want to get to the marina? Not today, buddy." I checked the gauges—half a tank of fuel on both engines. Huh. Weird. As we inched forward on one engine, I realized the real problem: marinas were closed. Classic. We found ourselves navigating with only one engine, trying to keep the boat from spinning in circles while Corey scouted for a place to dock.

After about 40 minutes of wild maneuvering, Corey found a private yacht club that would let us in—one engine or not. We were tired, hungry, and ready for a drink. So, after securing the boat, we made our way to the "The River Deck," a tiki bar with a live band. We sat at the bar, and Sami, the bartender, tall and charming, kept our drinks full while making us laugh. After a tense day of boating chaos, Sami's humor and her delicious margaritas and sodas were exactly what we needed. We decided she won our contest to find the most personable bartender on that trip. Sami won. After soaking in the atmosphere, we returned to the boat around 10:30 p.m. and slept hard, knowing we'd be up early for a mechanic's visit. The next morning, Samuel, the mechanic, arrived promptly at 11 a.m. and began his investigation. Turns out, the issue was a fuel line switcheroo from the Bahamas. Somehow, the starboard fuel tank was empty, but the gauge read half. Weird, right? After several hours of head-scratching, Samuel got the engines roaring at 6:30

p.m., and off he went. The owner was paying him so we gave him $100 for his trouble. A real pro.

By then, it was too late for anything except food and sleep. And guess where we went? Yep, The River Deck again. Sami was there, and the margaritas (mine being a virgin) tasted even better the second time around.

The next day, both engines started without issue, and we made our way to St. Augustine for a fuel stop. As we cruised north, we were treated to a pod of dolphins following us. It felt like they were saying, "Hey, you guys are doing okay!" But then, the ocean turned a little rough. I wanted to go faster, but the boat was like, "Nope, not today." We slowed down to 18 mph, soaking wet from the spray, as the boat somehow handled it all like a pro.

Eventually, we made it to Amelia Island. We topped off the fuel and headed into Fernandina Harbor Marina for the night. We had a much-needed meal in town and left at the sun up.

Eventually, we pulled into Tybee Island, Georgia, and found a quaint little restaurant called Bubba Gumbos. The food was fantastic—spicy shrimp, hush puppies with flavored butter, and the best apple cobbler I've ever had. The locals were friendly, and the stories of "Just Right," a boat that slammed into docks one morning because the captain wasn't sober, made me laugh harder than I'd laughed in days.

I found myself in a peculiar situation in Georgia, where I was trying to buy a T-shirt from Jules Salty Grub and Island Pub. Long story short, I waited 45 minutes to buy the shirt, because no one would take my money. I was convinced I was going to have to pay for it on the boat in the middle of the night. No one came after me, but I was not proud of that moment.

We wrapped up the night with another wild boat adventure and a trip to Charleston, SC, where I finally had the most palatable shrimp and grits I'd ever had (though I'm still not a fan of grits). By the time we made it to Bald Head Island, we had encountered everything from spoiled private school kids to the greatest dive bar bartender.

The next morning, we fueled up and began heading toward Morehead City. Our boat, a Sea Ray, wasn't exactly built for the rough seas we encountered, and our worst meal of the trip came in the form of something called the "Sanitary Fish Market and Restaurant." Spoiler alert: it wasn't sanitary, and it wasn't good. I left without finishing my meal, something I rarely do—except when it's as bad as that.

But the real adventure began when we crossed Albemarle Sound. It's shallow. It's windy. It's about as pleasant as a family reunion with that one uncle who insists on telling that story. The boat was salty from the spray, and as we navigated, it was literally trying to turn us around.

A highlight of this trip was our stop in Coinjock, North Carolina, a great place with the best prime rib in the state. Through word-of-mouth advertising, it has become a popular stopover for boaters in the know.

From bad meals and clueless dockhands to dolphin pods and one engine trying to sabotage us, it was the kind of trip that could only be made on a boat. A 48-foot yacht, to be exact. And in the end, I'd learned a lot: about boating, Southern hospitality, and the importance of margaritas and good T-shirts.

The journey had been a test of endurance, skill, and, above all, patience. We earned every mile from Virginia's sundrenched waters to Hell's Gate's swirling currents. A sense of finality hung in the air in the last stretch of the journey. The Sea Ray had carried us nearly 1,300 miles, each wave, gust of wind, and shifting tide bringing us closer to our destination.

The night had stretched behind us when we entered the mouth of Point Judith Harbor in Rhode Island. The full moon reflected off the water, casting a silver shimmer across the sound. The rhythmic hum of the engines had become second nature, the steady motion almost soothing as Corey and I traded shifts at the wheel. The world was calm, and for the first time in days, the stress of the journey melted away. There were no more tight docks, ferries to dodge, or unseen obstacles lurking beneath the surface. Just open water and a quiet horizon.

As dawn broke over Rhode Island Sound, we made our way into the gap at Point Judith, our vessel cutting through the water as the sun painted the sky orange and pink. Block Island, with its rocky shores and familiar silhouette, appeared on the horizon like a welcome friend.

But just as the last remnants of the night faded, a sudden flash of white in the distance caught my eye. A Coast Guard vessel, speeding toward us, its silhouette sharp against the morning light. I knew exactly what was about to happen. Point Judith had always been a training ground for the Coast Guard, and today, we were their "easy bait," as they liked to call it.

Within moments, the black-rubber boots of the crew clattered onto the deck, and the familiar, albeit slightly annoying, Coast Guard inspection began. Life jackets, fire extinguishers, bilge pumps, and flares—everything checked off, one item at a time. Of course, they found a few minor discrepancies. The flares were outdated, the bilge had a "small amount" of oil in it, and they were very particular about their scuff marks on the deck. The whole process felt like an unnecessary formality—checking off boxes while I stood there, half-distracted by the thought of the finish line so close I could almost touch it.

"Where are your documentation papers?" the lead officer asked.

I handed them over, and he inspected them with exaggerated care. The whole time, Corey kept cleaning below deck, unfazed by the interruption. Her calm during what had become a routine nuisance reminded me just how much she'd come to embody the spirit of this journey. It was all about resilience, attention to detail, and just getting things done— no matter the hurdles.

Once the inspection was complete, they gave us the "all clear" with their carbon copy—a reminder that some things never change even in the digital age. The Coast Guard's boat sped off, leaving us to clean up the Sea Ray, its engines now quiet and still in the shallows of the harbor.

We slowly made our way to the owner's dock. The tide was low, and as we neared the dock, one of the props scraped the bottom. The jolt sent a shiver down my spine. I tried to correct the course, but with the breeze picking up, I misjudged the maneuver and scraped the swim platform against one of the pilings. Damn it.

It was a small mishap in the grand scheme of things, but after 1,300 miles of flawless travel, it felt like a bitter end to an otherwise perfect journey. I winced, but I couldn't afford to dwell on it. The owner would have to pay for the repair—his boat, after all, his responsibility.

Corey and I quickly set to work, cleaning down the boat one last time. By now, the sun had fully risen, and the harbor around us had come to life with the bustle of fishermen and the occasional pleasure craft. In the distance, the owner's house came into view, and I knew that the long journey was nearly over.

We docked carefully, and as we secured the lines, I felt a mixture of relief and pride. We'd done it.

Later, as we washed our hands and grabbed our bags, I called Southwest to book our flights. The owner had points to use, and it seemed only fitting that we'd fly home in comfort after everything we'd experienced. Corey and I shared a quick, tired smile as we said goodbye to the Sea Ray. It had been our home for twelve days, and it had carried us through so much. Now, it was time to leave it behind and return to the world we'd left behind when we first set out on this adventure.

The journey was over. And though we had only made it from Stuart, Florida, to Rhode Island, it felt like we had crossed oceans. The long hours on the open water, the countless challenges, and the friends we'd met along the way all came together in this final, perfect moment.

What a ride. What an adventure. And, as always, one to remember.

Bubba Gumbo's—the best little dive with great gumbo, shrimp, hush puppies, and bartender.

My Wellcraft Quicksilver—took to Block Island many times.

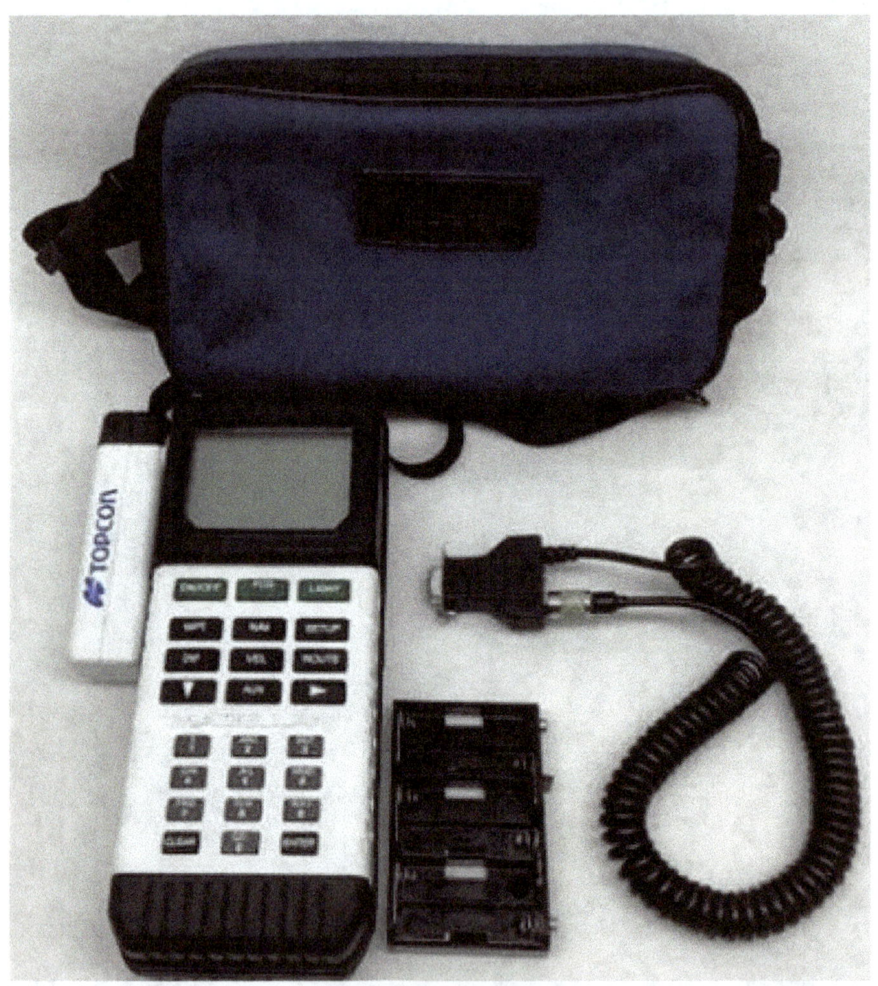

"A 1990 GPS was one of the first public ones. Only gave Lat/Lon and accurate to only 300 yards"

80-foot San Lorenzo from WPB to Hilton Head in SC. Lost a motor in a heavy storm.

Sami, the best bartender out of all our trips. Pretty, skilled, great conversationalist.

CHAPTER 13:
BATTLING THE ELEMENTS

There's an old saying among sailors that there are three kinds of people in this world: those who are alive, those who are dead, and those who are at sea. And after a lifetime spent plying this area of the world's gulfs, oceans, and waterways, I can attest to the truth of that sentiment. Because while boating has given me some of my life's greatest joys and most profound sensations of peace, it has also served up more than its fair share of white-knuckle moments and brushes with disaster. The sea, after all, is an unforgiving mistress— beautiful and beguiling one moment, deadly and capricious the next.

I've had more close calls and harrowing experiences out on the water than I can count. Each one is seared into my memory with a vividness that defies the passage of time. The sights, the sounds, the smells, the very taste of the salt spray on my lips all come rushing back with a clarity that can still set my heart racing and my palms sweating.

One that stands out was a delivery I made some years back, ferrying a 60-foot trawler from Newport to the Chesapeake. The forecast had been manageable when we set out—a bit of wind, some choppy seas, nothing we hadn't handled a hundred times before. But within a day of leaving port, things had deteriorated rapidly.

We found ourselves smack in the middle of a nasty storm, with winds howling at a steady 40 knots and gusts that pushed well into the 50s. The seas were an endless procession of heaving 8-foot swells, each one tipped with a frothy crown of white foam. The boat, for all her sturdy construction and advanced design, was getting positively hammered.

Down below, conditions were hellish. The constant motion had turned the cabin into a Tilt-a-Whirl of flying books, loose gear, and airborne crewmembers. Anything not battened down or bolted in place became a projectile weapon, careening off bulkheads and ricocheting around like a Super Ball in a squash court.

On deck, the situation was even worse. The force of the wind was like a physical thing, a malevolent presence that sought to rip the very wheel from your hands. The spindrift whipped across the wave tops, stinging any exposed skin like a thousand needles. And the noise - dear God, the noise.

The howling of the wind, the groaning of the cabin, the pounding of the waves against the hull combined into an unholy din that made communication all but impossible. You had to scream into someone's ear just to be heard, and even then, it was a 50/50 proposition.

Every so often, a rogue wave would rear up out of the maelstrom, towering over the boat like a liquid skyscraper. In those moments, time seemed to slow to a crawl. You'd watch the wall of water approach with a kind of detached fascination, your mind reeling at the sheer scale and power of the thing.

And then it would hit, and all hell would break loose. The bow would bury itself deep into the trough, the deck would tilt at a sickening angle, and for a few heart-stopping seconds, you'd wonder if the boat was ever going to come back up again. When she finally did, it was with a shuddering groan of protest, as if even she couldn't quite believe what was happening.

Through it all, the crew was a study in abject misery. Seasickness had claimed all but the hardiest among us, reducing grown men to quivering, retching wrecks. Even those who managed to keep their lunch down were hollow-eyed and haggard, the strain of constant vigilance and physical exertion taking its toll.

But what choice did we have? There was no turning back, no retreating to the safety of port. Our only option was to batten down the hatches, both literal and metaphorical, and endure. To keep putting one foot in front of the other, one hand over the other on the wheel, and keep the bow pointed into the maelstrom.

In moments like those, all your experience and training kick in. You don't have the luxury of fear or doubt or second-guessing. We focus on the task at hand with a singular intensity, breaking it down into its component parts. Trim the trim tabs. Mind the helm. Watch the waves. Check the bilge. Repeatedly, an endless loop of basic seamanship.

It's a curious thing, the way the mind works under duress. Time takes on an elastic quality, stretching and compressing in ways that defy logic. Details that would normally go unnoticed become imbued with a startling clarity - the way a coil of rope twists just so, the precise shade of green of a breaking wave, the glint of sunlight off a crewmate's rain-slicked follies.

At the same time, the bigger picture blurs and recedes, all your mental bandwidth consumed by the immediacy of the present moment. The past and the future cease to exist— there is only the now, the next wave, the next gust, the next crisis to be managed.

And manage them we did, one by one by one. We rode out the storm through sheer grit and determination, coaxing the boat through the worst of it with a combination of skill, luck, and white-knuckled resolve. It was, without question, one of the most challenging and exhausting ordeals of my nautical career.

But it was far from the only one. Over the years, I've had to contend with just about every flavor of maritime misfortune you can imagine. Engine failures, steering malfunctions, broken rudders, snapped rails, collisions with submerged objects—you name it, I've probably dealt with it at some point.

Each one presents its own unique set of challenges and demands its own brand of resourcefulness. When the engine conks out in the middle of the ocean, you can't exactly call AAA for a tow. You must make do with what you have on hand, rigging solutions out of spare parts, duct tape, and WD40.

I remember one time, on a delivery from Miami to Bimini, the gas boat's only alternator gave up the ghost halfway across the Gulf Stream. Without it, we had no way to charge the batteries and keep the electrical systems running. We were dead in the water, drifting on the current with no means of propulsion.

After a few minutes of creative cursing, I set to work. Using a length of spare rope and a pulley salvaged from an old block and tackle, I managed to rig up a makeshift connection between the engine and the alternator. It was crude and ugly, but it got the job done—we limped into port under our own power, the boat's heart stuttering but still beating.

When things go sideways out there, that's the key—you have to stay calm, assess the situation objectively, and methodically work on the problem. Panic is the enemy. It clouds your judgment, saps your energy, and invariably leads to poor decisions. The sea is an unforgiving taskmaster—she always demands a cool head and a steady hand.

You also must be decisive, even when the right course of action isn't entirely clear. When you're facing a crisis at sea, there's no room for hesitation or equivocation. Your crew is looking to you to lead, to make the tough calls, and get them to safety. Indecision can be just as deadly as poor seamanship.

I've had moments out there where I've had to make split-second decisions that carried life-or-death consequences. Do we heave to and ride out the storm, or try to outrun it? Do we attempt a repair, press on, or turn back and seek safe harbor? Do we risk a treacherous inlet in failing light or spend the night hove-to in open water?

In the end, you have to trust your gut and your experience, weigh the risks and rewards, and make the call. And then you have to own it, for better or for worse. Because when things go wrong out there, there's no one to blame but yourself. The sea doesn't grade on a curve.

Of course, sometimes even the best judgment and the most skilled seamanship aren't enough. There have been times when I've been truly overmatched by the conditions, when no amount of experience or expertise could keep the boat and crew safe.

In those moments, you must have the humility and the wisdom to know when you're beaten. To swallow your pride, hit the EPIRB (that's the Emergency Position Indicating Radio Beacon, for you landlubbers), call for help if you must, and abandon ship if necessary. It's a gut-wrenching decision, but sometimes it's the only one you can make.

I've been lucky—I've never had to take that step, though I've come close a time or two. But I know plenty of sailors who have, and to a man, they'll tell you it's the hardest thing they've ever had to do. Watching your boat slip beneath the waves, knowing you're leaving a part of yourself behind - it's a special kind of heartbreak.

But it beats the alternative. Because as much as we like to romanticize the notion of going down with the ship, the reality is that a dead captain is no good to anyone. Better to live to fight another day, to learn from your mistakes, and to come back stronger and wiser.

And mistakes, I've made my fair share. Every sailor has. It's how we learn, how we grow, how we become better at our craft. Each scare, each close call, teaches you something new —about the boat, about the sea, about yourself. I pride myself on learning something new each day, and there is never enough learning with a boat on the water. Take fog, for instance. It's one of the most insidious and disorienting phenomena a sailor can encounter. It creeps up on you with no warning, swallowing the horizon and turning the world into a featureless gray void. Sounds become muffled and distorted, and distances can be impossible to judge. Even the most familiar coastline can become a labyrinth of hidden dangers.

I've had occasions where the fog was so thick, I couldn't see the bow of my own boat from the cockpit. Navigating through soup like that is an exercise of pure faith—faith in your instruments, charts, and abilities. You must trust that you know where you are and where you're going, even when instinct tells you otherwise.

It can play tricks on your mind, too. More than once, I've found myself jumping at shadows, convinced I've seen another vessel looming out of the murk, only to realize it was a trick of the light and my own overactive imagination. The mind can be your worst enemy in moments like that.

But as treacherous as fog can be, it's far from the only adversary a sailor has to contend with. I've faced down lightning storms that lit up the night sky like a strobe light, waterspouts that danced and spun across the wave tops like malevolent ballerinas, winds that screamed through the rigging with a banshee's wail.

I've dealt with crushing fatigue, the kind that turns your limbs to lead and your thoughts to molasses. I've faced equipment failures that left me adrift and alone, forced to rely on my wits and my luck to see me through. I've tended to crewmembers stricken with everything from seasickness to appendicitis, playing doctor and nursemaid in rolling seas.

And through it all, I've come to understand one fundamental truth about life on the water: that the sea is the ultimate equalizer. It doesn't care about your pedigree, net worth, status, or station. All it cares about is your ability to adapt, to endure, to persevere in the face of adversity.

In a sense, I suppose that's part of the allure of boating— the challenge of pitting yourself against the elements and coming out the other side. There's a certain primal satisfaction in making it to port safely after a white-knuckled ordeal, in knowing that you've stared down the worst that Mother Nature can throw at you and lived to tell the tale.

But I never lose sight of who's really in charge out there. The sea is a harsh mistress, fickle and unforgiving. She'll test you in ways you never thought possible, pushing you to the very limits of your endurance and beyond. And if you're not careful and let your guard down for even a moment, she'll claim you as her own.

I've seen it happen more times than I care to remember. Good sailors, skilled and experienced, who made one small mistake or had one stroke of bad luck and paid for it with their lives. The sea doesn't discriminate, and she doesn't give second chances.

That's why preparation is so crucial. Before every voyage, I go over the boat with a fine-toothed comb, checking and double-checking every system and equipment. I study the charts and the forecasts obsessively, trying to anticipate every possible contingency. I drill my crew on emergency procedures until they can do them in their sleep.

Because when things start to go sideways out there, when the waves are crashing over the bow, and the wind is howling in your ears, you don't have time to think. You must act, quickly and decisively, relying on muscle memory and ingrained instinct to see you through.

That's where experience comes in. Every old salt has their war stories, their tales of high seas and close calls. And each one is a reminder of just how fragile and insignificant we are in the face of nature's fury. But they're also a testament to the indomitable human spirit, to our ability to confront the unknown and the unconquerable and come out on the other side. To look fear in the face and refuse to blink, to stare down the abyss and step forward anyway.

It also helps to have a good crew, which is why I'd like to say a few words about Corey. She was the kind of deckhand you'd wish you could clone and just keep around forever. Let me paint you a picture: Corey is the type of person who could outmaneuver, out-fix, and out-sail most of the guys I've had on deck, all while wearing the same pair of scuffed sneakers she's had since high school. And don't get me started on how she can handle a 60-foot boat in three-foot seas with the precision of a surgeon. Meanwhile, I'm over here, gripping the wheel like it's my last day on Earth, and Corey's casually adjusting the fenders as if it's no big deal.

She wasn't just any deckhand, though. Oh, no. She was my co-captain in the making, working her way toward that 100ton license with the kind of tenacity that would make even the toughest captains nod in approval. We did a fair amount of boat deliveries together, and let me tell you, Corey knew more about engines, electronics, and the finer points of navigation than most men with 20 years in the biz. When the engine sputtered, Corey didn't panic, and she just went to work. And if something was broken, she fixed it, usually before I even had a chance to Google how to do it myself.

But, as with all good things, there comes a time when paths diverge. Corey moved on to other adventures, and I had to start the hunt for a new mate. But that doesn't mean I'm not going to miss her. I'll miss the way she could fix a rope knot like she was weaving a tapestry. I'll miss her endless patience when I was trying to get the boat into a slip and her calm voice on the radio when things got chaotic. I'll miss her — let's just say — "colorful" commentary during those long shifts. But most of all, I'll miss having a co-captain who could anticipate my every move, making the job look easy.

That was Corey—a deckhand, a co-captain, a navigator, and a damn good friend. You don't burn bridges with people like her. You just hope that your paths cross again somewhere down the road — preferably with a boat between us. Until then, I'll be on the lookout for the next Corey, though I'll be hard-pressed to find someone who can fill her boots (which, let's be honest, probably have a few more miles on them than mine).

In the end, it's all about having the courage to leave the shore's safety, embrace the challenge of the unknown, and discover what lies beyond the horizon. The sea has been my greatest teacher, reminding me of my limitations and showcasing the human spirit's incredible resilience.

I'm grateful for the lessons, memories, and scars that come with this journey. Life on the water is about facing struggles, discovering your true strength, and living on your own terms. It's about the bonds created in shared adversity.

To my fellow sailors, keep pushing forward against the waves and writing your stories of adventure. Regardless of the challenges, return to the sea for the beauty and joy of it all. If you go slow like a pro, prepare and don't panic, you'll come out on top. That's what being alive is about—facing fear and uncertainty with resolve. The sailor's creed unites us in our journey. Here's to the mariners who brave storms and seek new horizons. May your sails be full and your journeys rewarding because it's all about the journey and the spirit that drives us into the unknown.

Rough seas off the Chesapeake. Not a pleasant time for anyone.

CHAPTER 14:
LEGACIES AND REFLECTIONS

As I sit here, salt crusting my skin after a long day on the water, I can't help but reflect on the incredible role that boating and the sea have played in my life. It's not just a hobby or even a career; it's an integral part of who I am, as essential to my being as the blood coursing through my veins. The ocean is in my DNA, and I wouldn't have it any other way.

Some of my earliest and most formative memories revolve around the water. It's been my playground, my refuge, my greatest teacher, and my most enduring muse. From those tentative steps into the surf as a boy to the countless hours spent at the helm chasing the horizon, the sea has shaped me in profound and immeasurable ways.

I often think back to the wisdom my father imparted, advice that has served me well not just in boating, but in business and in life. "Son," he used to say, "when you face a challenge in your boat or life, the best thing you can do is step back, calm down, and think of all the possible scenarios and outcomes. The right one will eventually surface or reveal itself."

Dad passed away in 2005, but his words live on, a guiding light through stormy seas. Ironically, he wasn't much of a boater himself—the mere mention of a ferry ride was enough to turn his stomach. But he understood the principles of navigation, both literal and metaphorical.

I sure do miss that guy, but his words of wisdom continue to serve me well.

Boating has given me so much over the years—freedom, joy, adventure, purpose, humility, self-reliance, and some of the greatest friendships a man could ask for. It has taught me to read the skies, to improvise repairs with little more than duct tape and a prayer, and to stare down my fears with a steady hand on the wheel.

But perhaps more than anything, it's instilled in me a profound respect for the raw power and beauty of the natural world, and an abiding sense of my own smallness in the grand scheme of things. Out there on the waves, you quickly learn that you're not the master of the universe. The sea is the boss, and she'll make a believer out of you one way or another.

So many of the qualities I value most in myself—resilience, resourcefulness, courage, calm in the face of adversity—have been forged and tempered through my time on the water. The sea has a way of stripping away pretense and revealing who you really are, for better or worse. It's the great equalizer and the ultimate truth-teller. You can't bluff your way through a gale or fast-talk a 10-foot swell.

But for all its challenges, boating has also given me an incredible sense of community and shared passion. Some of my dearest and most enduring friendships were forged not in a boardroom or on a golf course but over a rail or a helm, united by our love of the wind and the waves. The culture of boating is one of generosity, camaraderie, and mutual care. We look out for each other out there because we know all too well what it takes and what's at stake.

I feel so deeply fortunate to have been able to turn my life's greatest passion into my livelihood. Not everyone gets to do that: wake up every day and do what sets their soul on fire. The opportunity to share my love of the water with others and help them build their skills and confidence has been an incredible gift and a profound responsibility.

My greatest hope is that, in some small way, the stories I've told and the experiences I've shared might inspire others to chase their dreams, push their boundaries, and find their own slice of blue-sky freedom. If I can impart even a fraction of the joy, the wonder, and the sense of possibility that boating has given me, I'll consider it a life well-lived.

I also hope that through my work and my advocacy, I've helped foster a greater appreciation and stewardship of our oceans and waterways. The sea is a gift, but it's also a responsibility. We're all just temporary passengers on this big blue marble, and it's on us to ensure that the waters remain clean, healthy, and teeming with life for generations to come.

As I look to the future, I know that time and tide wait for no man. The years slip by like waves under the keel, and the body that once leaped into the spray with abandon now creaks and groans like an old wooden hull. But even as age exacts its inevitable toll, I know that the sea will always be a part of me, as much as my love for my family or the blood in my veins.

It's brought me full circle, from a wide-eyed boy marveling at the vastness of the ocean to a weathered old salt content to spend his days puttering around the harbor. And through it all, through the storms and the calms, the triumphs and the trials, I'm so deeply grateful—for a loving wife who's been my anchor, for loyal friends who've crewed with me through thick and thin, for a strong mind and body that have allowed me to do what I love for so long, and for a lifetime spent in pursuit of something greater than myself.

The horizon still beckons, and my course remains true. If there's a breeze in my sail and a gleam in my eye, I'll be scanning the charts and plotting my next adventure. Because, in the end, that's what a life well-lived is all about—chasing your passions, making a difference, leaving the world a little better than you found it.

And if someday, somewhere, a starry-eyed kid leaves through these pages and sees a glimmer of their dreams and possibilities reflected in them? Well, that'll be the greatest legacy of all.

Some of the boating crew from Block Island eating as we often did. A BIG GROUP enjoying life.

A small sampling of the group of boaters in Florida. Great friends.

FISHERMAN'S PRAYER

Oh, Lord, your sea is so large, and my boat is so small.

Please watch over me.

The ease of the ocean, rolling waves, magnificent night sky: these are just some of the things that have gotten me hooked on the sea. There is nothing like watching a pod of over 200 porpoises pass by your boat, or a lone whale, following your yacht, curious as to what it is. And when that whale breaches, it is the most fascinating thing to see. At night on the water, there are no man-made lights to dim the gorgeous stars and moon. I follow with my night vision and make my way through a blue-green bioluminescence that comes to the surface on a calm night. When the boat or a slight breeze ripples the water, it turns into the colors of a fairytale. The water, when it's not playing with you, is a wonderful fascination God made, and you can't remember ever seeing the ocean like this.